"Was that to make the engagement seem more real?" Ellie asked.

The question came out as a whisper. She regretted it a second later, sure that he would use it as an excuse to switch back to the cool, in-control Derrick she'd met that first night.

He smiled down at her. "Do you think there are cameras in here?"

"I meant were you trying to get me accustomed to kissing you."

"I kissed you because I wanted to kiss you." He skimmed his thumb over her lower lip. "For the record, fake engagement or not, I don't want you to kiss me unless you want to."

"We seem to be stepping into dangerous territory."

"Agreed." He cupped her cheek and his fingers slipped into her hair. The simple touch, so light, felt so good...and so scary.

This was fake. This was about saving her brother and restoring Derrick's reputation.

That was all it could be.

* * *

Pregnant by the CEO is part of
The Jameson Heirs series—

They'll do anything to save the
family business—even fall in love!

Dear Reader,

I love to read about big, messy families. On the outside they're successful, confident and together. On the inside? Ugh.

The Jameson brothers fit this description perfectly. They are a tad dysfunctional, not great with interpersonal skills, estranged from their very troublesome dad, but fiercely loyal to each other. Set in Washington, DC, and the Virginia horse country, the books will follow each brother as he figures out that money, prestige and a Kennedy-like following don't impress the woman he can't forget.

First up—big brother Derrick. He runs the family business and has a bit of a problem with his public image. He's looking to Ellie Gold to help him with that. But does he ask? Not exactly. He bulldozes his way into her life with the help of a gossip site and, well, things are a bit bumpy...

I hope you enjoy Derrick and Ellie's story, and all the Jameson heirs!

Happy reading!

HelenKay

HELENKAY DIMON

——

PREGNANT BY THE CEO

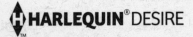

HARLEQUIN® DESIRE

Recycling programs
for this product may
not exist in your area.

ISBN-13: 978-1-335-97128-9

Pregnant by the CEO

Copyright © 2018 by HelenKay Dimon

This edition published by arrangement with Harlequin Books S.A.

For questions and comments about the quality of this book, please contact us at CustomerService@Harlequin.com.

Printed in U.S.A.

HelenKay Dimon is a divorce lawyer turned full-time author. Her bestselling and award-winning books have been showcased in numerous publications, including the *Washington Post* and *Cosmopolitan*. She is an RT Reviewers' Choice Award winner and has been a finalist for the Romance Writers of America's RITA® Award multiple times. This is her first Harlequin Desire novel.

Books by HelenKay Dimon

Harlequin Intrigue

Corcoran Team: Bulletproof Bachelors

Cornered
Sheltered
Tamed

Corcoran Team

Fearless
Ruthless
Relentless
Lawless
Traceless

Mystery Men

Under the Gun
Guns and the Girl Next Door
Gunning for Trouble
Locked and Loaded
The Big Guns

Visit her Author Profile page at Harlequin.com, or helenkaydimon.com, for more titles.

One

The DC Insider: Rumor has it Washington, DC's most eligible and notoriously difficult bachelor—the man named the Insider's *Hottest Ticket in Town for three years running—might finally be off the market. All that talk about bad security and bad management? Could be a disgruntled baby brother getting even with his sister's new beau. When asked about a supposed secret girlfriend and her meddlesome brother, hotshot businessman Derrick Jameson would only say, "Ellie Gold is lovely." Sounds like an admission to us. Stay tuned.*

Ellie Gold had never punched anyone before, but she vowed to end that lifelong streak right now.

Wearing the only cocktail dress she owned, simple

and black, with a matching black lace overlay, and spiky heels that made her arches ache, she stepped into the private dining room on the top floor of the historic Hay-Adams Hotel named, interestingly enough, the Top of the Hay.

For a second the anger choking her brain cleared. Her breath hitched as her gaze wandered around the sparkling space with the fancy chandeliers and cream-colored walls. Only the business people milling around with death grips on their drinks, all looking awkward and out of place in their navy suits, threatened to ruin the fairy-tale moment.

French doors lined the outer walls and vaulted skylights soared above her. She stretched up on tiptoe to peek around more than one set of shoulders to the stunning view of the White House below.

Her balance faltered and she might have landed headfirst in a nearby tray of champagne glasses but fingers wrapped around her elbow and steadied her. She glanced up to say thank-you and saw a face… *his* face.

Derrick Jameson, the oldest son of a vast empire that included everything from commercial real estate in Washington, DC, to a prize-winning horse farm in the Virginia countryside. The guy who excelled at making her life miserable.

Just seeing him made her forget how to spell. She wasn't all that sure she could recite the alphabet if pressed, either. She wanted to blame the fury flowing through her, but even she had to admit that might not be the real reason for her hottie-induced speech lapse.

She'd researched Derrick before tonight, reading online in stories that droned on about his money and dating life. But seeing him up close? No one had prepared her for that.

The black hair and striking light brown eyes. She'd read about his family background and picked up on the subtle hint of Japanese heritage passed on from his maternal grandmother. The firm chin. Those shoulders.

The features combined into a potent package of tall, dark and delicious. He gave off a confident vibe. In control and assessing. But his unspoken determination to destroy her reputation and rip her family apart marred her appreciation of his pretty face.

"Ms. Gold." He nodded and threw in a little smile for a group of people walking past him. "I didn't expect to see you at a business function."

Her voice came back to her in a rush. So did the rage swirling in her gut. "Interesting tactic."

"Excuse me?"

"That charming thing you're doing?" She leaned in closer and dropped her voice to a whisper, ignoring how good he smelled. "I'm not buying it."

He continued to hold her arm. Not in a tight grip. No, his thumb brushed back and forth over her bare skin in a gentle caress, as if trying to soothe her. The guy seemed oblivious to the fact that he was the one causing her stress. Well, him and everyone and everything else in her life.

He might not know it but she hovered right on the edge and his decisions kept shoving her closer to the abyss. Her baby brother, Noah, was in a strange emotional downward spiral, all thanks to Derrick and his claims about Noah stealing from him.

She'd practically raised Noah after their parents

died in a car crash. He wasn't easy, but he wasn't a thief. Her brother had been argumentative and frustrated back then, much more so than other kids. She'd dragged him to a specialist, who diagnosed him with oppositional defiant disorder, something she'd never even heard of before that moment.

She'd scraped together the money for the therapies not covered by insurance. But even now, at times of stress or when he felt cornered, the flashes of anger would come back and he'd buck authority. Something about Derrick had Noah's negative behavior kicking to the surface again.

The worst part was that Noah didn't even see it. She did. She'd watched him make bad choices as a kid, tried to help him to the point where she'd sacrificed her personal life to spend all of her extra time with him. The idea that his issues were resurging now, at twenty, deflated her.

She'd deal with that later. Right now she needed to handle Derrick.

"This is serious." Serious enough for her to track him down through a series of calls to his office.

"Is it?" Amusement filled his voice as he handed her his glass of champagne.

She couldn't think of anything more annoying than that welcoming lilt to his voice. The whole fake-charming scene threw her off. She didn't realize he had shifted and moved them toward the elevators until she looked around the room and saw the space between them and the rest of the party.

She didn't know if this was a rich guy's way of escorting her out of the building or something else. Either way, she was not ready to be dismissed. There was too much at stake for her to give up now. "Mr. Jameson, I—"

"Derrick."

She'd investigated Derrick's business when her baby brother got a job there seven months ago. At first, Noah had talked about Derrick in a nonstop cycle of hero worship. His enthusiasm had rubbed off on her. She'd clicked on every photo of him. Let her mind wander, tried to imagine what it might be like to see that shockingly handsome face close up.

Now she knew.

She worked in human resources up until six weeks ago. She hadn't reached management level yet. The Jameson family was the equivalent of DC royalty. She didn't move in their world. She also possessed a general distrust of people who rolled around in that kind of money. But Noah had been impressed. And, up until that point in his life, almost *nothing* had impressed her brilliant but moody brother.

In theory, Derrick was more mature and reasonable than her brother. But thanks to this gossip site silliness she wasn't totally convinced that was true.

"The *DC Insider* posted a note about us." The comment rolled out of her mouth as if it made any sense. She still couldn't believe she had to confront him about this.

For a second Derrick stared at her, not saying a word, then he nodded. "I know."

Words backed up in her brain until she finally pushed them out. "What kind of response is that?"

"My name is in the social column because I allowed it to be there."

Good grief. "Are you kidding?"

He frowned at her. "No."

"I'm thinking people have let you get away with nonsense for far too long." When he started to pipe in, she talked right over him. "I mean, really. Do you know how condescending you sound?"

This time he studied her. She could feel him assessing and reordering his strategy as they talked.

"I called you *lovely* in that *Insider* quote, if that helps," he said.

It took a second for her brain to catch up again. She silently blamed all the people in suits standing around, staring at them and whispering, but she worried his smooth tone might be the *real* issue with her concentration. "It doesn't, and that's not the point."

"Should I have used a different word?"

His focus on vocabulary made her head pound. She shifted until she put her back to most of the room. Maybe not seeing the gawkers would help. "Stop talking."

He made a sound that came close to a growl. "People don't usually speak to me that way."

"Which is probably part of the problem here." She'd never worked in a classroom but her mother had. Ellie called up that disappointed-fifth-grade-teacher tone without even trying. "Okay, so you're admitting you planted the article?"

"Of course."

The champagne sloshed over the side of her glass. "The one about me?"

Because that was the point. She came there to pry the truth out of him about the planted story, maybe put him on the defensive. He ruined her plans by admitting to spreading the gossip, like it was no big deal.

He slipped the flute out of her fingers and put it on the small table behind him. "Technically, the story is about me."

She inhaled, trying to bring some air into her lungs and refresh her brain cells. She refused to get lost in his words or have a "him" versus "them" fight because she had the very clear sense confusing wordplay was one of the ways he won arguments. "Okay, why do it?"

"To change the public conversation from your brother's false allegations while I figure out what he did with the money that is now missing from my business accounts." Derrick answered without blinking, following their conversation with ease as it bounced around.

She decided to ignore the money part for now. "But you named me as your...well, I guess as the woman you're dating?"

"That's right."

She had no idea what to think about that nonchalant response. "We don't even know each other. Why would you think that's okay?"

"My *business* is the most important thing to me."

She didn't try to hide her wince at his sudden stern tone. "My *brother* is the most important thing to me."

"Wrong answer, Ellie."

Was he really making a tsking sound? "What is wrong with you?"

"I have two brothers, both adults," Derrick explained with all the emotion of someone reading a recipe. "They take care of themselves. I take care of me and the business."

"That's cold...bloodless."

He actually smiled. "Is it possible you're the one with the confused priorities?"

She swallowed a gasp, along with a bit of her anger and possibly some of her dignity. The whole conversation was ridiculous but she could not tear herself away from him...not yet.

"Let me get this straight. A perpetual bachelor and notorious ladies' man who is being trolled on the internet by my little brother in his antibusiness videos is giving me advice on interpersonal relationships?" She wanted to sigh, throw things. "Listen, Mr. Jameson."

"It's still Derrick."

The way he stayed calm made her temper spike even more. The heat rose inside her and flooded her cheeks with every controlled word he uttered. She refused to believe the sudden need for a fan had anything to do with his perfect face or that sexy smile. Not that she found either all that appealing. "Do not mention my name to anyone ever again."

"Now, Ellie." His eyes narrowed. "You don't think that's maybe—just a little—extreme."

Apparently she was not the only one familiar with the teacher tone. He threw it out there and nailed her with it. As if she needed another reason to dislike him. "Leave my brother alone."

"When your brother comes clean and then backs off those videos, I will."

"You're a grown-up."

"So is he." Derrick leaned in close enough for his warm breath to brush her cheek. "My suggestion to you is that you start treating him like one."

"I'm not kidding around."

His eyes traveled over her face, lingering on her mouth. "I can see that."

She fought off the tremor moving through her. "Leave me out of your games."

Before he could say anything else or touch her again, she slipped around him and through the crowd of people heading toward them. Kept going until she got on the elevator and watched the doors close on his smiling face. Getting her breathing to return to normal and the image of his face to disappear from her mind took longer.

An hour later Ellie poured a glass of red wine as she kicked off her stupid heels. Thanks to a bout of storming and muttering, she'd wasted most of her energy and hadn't made it to her apartment. She needed to vent and that meant taking the Metro to her best friend's condo instead.

Vanessa McAllister's one-bedroom place was small but cozy. Light bounced off the bright yellow walls. During the day, the sun beamed in from the large window at the far end of the living room.

A steady beat of background conversation came from the television. Ellie had no idea what show was on and didn't care. Vanessa didn't appear to, either.

Of course, very little ruffled her. Between her navy career father and her French mother, Vanessa had been all over the world. She spoke a ridiculous number of languages that served her well in her job at the museum.

Ellie trusted Vanessa with any secret. They'd met in college and had been best friends ever since. They supported and cheered for each other. And right now, Vanessa was frowning.

She sat on the stool at her kitchen's breakfast bar. She sipped from her almost-empty glass of red wine as she scowled at the laptop screen in front of her. "Tell me again what happened at that fancy cocktail party."

The somewhat distant tone. That wasn't good.

Ellie was almost afraid to answer. She did, anyway. "I met Derrick Jameson and told him to back off."

The explanation sounded good. So strong. Just what Ellie wanted to be. After years of racing around, trying to keep every ball in the air and failing most of the time, Ellie wanted to be in control of her life and not running behind it, trying to catch up.

Vanessa tapped on the keyboard. "Uh-huh."

Yeah, not good. "What does that response mean?"

"Did you happen to see a photographer while you were there?" Vanessa sat straighter and waved her hand in the air. "Forget it. I'll just go ahead and read it to you before you explode."

Ellie dropped the paper napkin she was twisting in her fingers. "Wait, read what?"

"The latest from that *Insider* site."

"No." Ellie's stomach fell. She could have sworn it hit the floor.

"'Derrick Jameson and Ellie Gold made an official appearance together at the swanky Hay-Adams Hotel tonight. No word on whether they got a room, but they did leave the business party one right after the other, making more than one partygoer wonder if Derrick sprang for the presidential suite…'"

Silence screamed through the room. Ellie could feel it hammering in her head as it rumbled through her.

"Okay." Vanessa cleared her throat. "So, that happened."

"It did *not* happen." Ellie reached over and turned the laptop to face her. "We argued. We fought."

She started tapping random keys. Anything to make that now familiar *Insider* website disappear.

"Wait, go back. There's a photo." Vanessa swatted Ellie's hand away then leaned in and pointed at the screen. "Why does it look like you're hanging on his arm?"

As if Ellie could deny it. The evidence, even though it didn't show the whole story, was right there. Her pressing against him, looking up at him. Anyone seeing this would believe they were having an intimate chat.

"That's not… I was just…" The words clogged her throat in the rush to get them out. "I'm going to kill him."

Vanessa winced. "You can't think that he—"

"Of course he planted this. I'm his PR plan." And he wasn't even trying to hide it. He'd been very clear. She just hadn't realized he'd turned it on full-time.

Vanessa made a humming sound. "He really is cute."

"Don't."

"But clearly a gigantic ass." Vanessa's voice sounded harsher that time.

"Better." But still not good enough. Ellie wanted to forget all about his smug face.

"Hating him doesn't fix the Noah situation," Vanessa said, being far too reasonable for the moment.

"Or help with my income issue or get my life under control. Yeah, I know."

Vanessa's shoulders fell as she sighed. "I can give you money, or move in here with me and don't pay rent for a few months. Give yourself a financial break."

"I can't."

"You can." Vanessa made a grumbling sound as she said something under her breath that wasn't quite clear. "I'm thinking about stuffing twenties into your purse while you're not looking."

With that, Ellie felt some of the Derrick-related anger drain away. She reached over and gave her friend's arm a quick squeeze. "You're awesome and I love you, but this is bigger than a short-term money problem. It's like everything is spinning and I can't make it stop." Even now her life choices ran through her head as she questioned each one. "I still can't believe I got fired for something that wasn't my fault."

"So, take it back." Vanessa grabbed the bottle and refilled her glass. "Control, I mean. Start with one thing. You take a small piece, conquer that and then move on."

The advice rolled around in Ellie's head until it took hold. She knew exactly which battle to wage first. "Right. Derrick Jameson."

"Um, no. I was thinking more like you could get a temp job and rebuild." Vanessa topped off Ellie's glass. "A guy like Jameson is not easily managed. Forget him. Handle what *you* need first."

The suggestion made sense but Ellie couldn't survive that way. She'd spent so much of her life fixing things. First, for her father, who had one pipe dream after another, and her mother, who had fought to keep them together as a family. Then for her brother. She didn't have the energy left to tackle straightening out her life, but she would. Later. Once she'd dealt with Derrick and Noah was back on track. "I have to handle these other pieces first."

Vanessa shook her head. "Ellie, you can't fix everything."

"I can fix this. If Derrick Jameson wants a battle, he's going to get one."

Two

The DC Insider: *The hottest romance in town just got more interesting. Ever wonder what happens when the lady in question calls our office to insist there is no romance? Well, we call the gentlemen for his comment. And Derrick Jameson did not disappoint. The usually demanding businessman chuckled and said, "You should listen to Ellie. I enjoy acquiescing to her." These two are never dull.*

She'd been summoned.

The call came at a little after nine the next morning. Ellie debated ignoring it. She wasn't exactly the type to jump when a man ordered, but then Derrick was no ordinary man. He seemed to enjoy ticking her off.

Yet there she was, two hours later, walking along

a long hallway on the fifteenth floor of the Jameson Industries' office building. Pristine white walls surrounded her as her heels clicked against the polished hardwood floors. People moved in and out and around cubicle walls. They carried stacks of papers and shuffled with a sense of urgency.

She missed the energy of a busy office. Insurance underwriting wasn't the most exciting topic but she'd worked in human resources, slowly taking on more responsibility. She loved coming into a pile of files waiting on her desk each morning and solving problems.

Everything went fine until the big boss took an overactive interest in her. She'd done everything she'd been trained to do. Documented his behavior. She'd known how hard it was to report that sort of thing up the chain of command without becoming the subject of gossip. Before her boss made his move she'd set up a system to handle the concerns. Then she got fired before she could implement it.

The attorney she contacted about the firing but could barely afford said she had a good case. But her former boss had the resources to drag the thing out and exhaust her.

She tried not to think about that as two men headed straight for her. She slipped to the side, banging into the wall and knocking the corner of a painting. One that likely cost more than her car. After that, one more turn and she moved into a quieter part of the floor. No one scurried here.

Sleek furniture made of unblemished leather with shiny chrome accents filled the open reception area. That, and a desk covered with piles of files, was all that stood between her and a set of closed double doors. Those and the guy next to her. She couldn't remember her escort's name, wasn't even sure he'd offered it.

Before she could ask, he reached out and knocked on the door to the right in front of them. One brisk thwack then he opened it. Even gestured for her to step inside in front of him.

No, thank you.

Her legs refused to move, anyway. The threshold seemed innocent enough, but the man on the other side was not. Every inch of this place screamed money. Something she'd never had enough of and worked liked crazy to stockpile in case her life hit a bump... just as it had. More like a Himalayan mountain, but still.

She couldn't see Derrick at the moment, but she did have an unrestricted view of his desk. The thing had to be eight feet long. Formidable, like the man who sat at it.

She refused to go one step further. Decided to call out instead. "What do you want?"

"Come inside," the faceless voice said from some hidden corner of the office.

She noted the deep and commanding tone. Yeah, this was going to be a quick meeting.

"I'm fine here," she said.

The security guy put his hand over his mouth to cover what sounded like a fake cough. He hesitated a second before saying anything. "You really should obey him."

Apparently she'd gotten off the elevator and stepped back a century. "Did you use the word *obey*?"

"Don't fight with Jackson. It's me you want," Derrick said, still without making an appearance.

She glanced at the man looming next to her. He stood well over six feet with brown hair and a lean athletic build. Attractive in a liked-to-run-along-the-Potomac sort of way, he looked far too amused by what was happening. "Is Jackson your first name or last?"

Before he could answer, Derrick stepped out of the room off to the side of his office and into the doorway. Hovered right in front of her. He nodded as a small smile played on the corner of his mouth. "Ellie, it's good to see you again."

The warmth in his eyes. That tone. A strange dizziness slammed into her when he got close. No way was she being reeled in by that charm thing he seemed to have flicked on. Nope, she knew better.

She managed a nod. "Mr. Jameson."

"Come inside. Despite our argument last night, we have a lot to discuss." He swept a hand toward the inside of his oversize corner office.

The very real sense she was out of her league slammed into her. "What would you do if I said no?"

He frowned. "Why would you?"

"You have this guy following me around the hallways…no offense." She winced as she glanced at Jackson before looking at Derrick again. "Then there's the part where you ordered me to come here. Today. Right now."

"Ten minutes ago."

"What?"

"I *asked* you to meet with me ten minutes ago. I assumed you being late was some sort of power play.

Unless you have a problem with tardiness. If so, we'll need to work on that."

She glanced at Jackson again. "Is he serious?"

Jackson nodded. "Almost always."

"Ellie." That's it. Derrick just said her name then turned and walked across the room, stopping next to his desk.

"Your manners need some work." She didn't bother mumbling as she followed him. If he wasn't going to be subtle, neither was she.

"So I've been told."

"Then there's the very real sense you're setting me up." Not so much a sense as a fact. If he planted one rumor, he could plant many. And that seemed to be his intent.

"How so?" He had the nerve to look confused. She refused to believe he was that clueless.

"I complain about a story on the internet about us and suddenly there's a photo of us up there, complete with a new quote from you." An annoying quote. One that didn't say anything yet managed to say a lot. "I called them and denied that we were together and you…actually, I don't know what you were doing when you talked to the *Insider*."

"I was being a gentleman."

She took a few steps. Hovering there in his office gave her confidence. "You mean the I-don't-kiss-and-tell thing? Oh, please. You were toying with them because it amused you."

"Admittedly, I'm not often at a loss for words, but I'm not sure what to say to that comment."

"You could admit you set me up to be featured on

the *Insider*. Again." The sound of a cough and rustling had her turning around.

Jackson stood there with his attention focused on Derrick. "Do you need anything from me, sir?"

"No, but it would be wise to stay close by in the hall in case Ms. Gold brought a weapon."

She had forgotten poor Jackson was still there. Hearing the door click behind her as he left, she tried not to fidget. Now it was the two of them temporarily trapped in a room bigger than her entire apartment.

Rather than retreat, she stepped forward. Followed Derrick's trail until she stood on the opposite side of his desk and watched him slip into his chair. "As if I could have gotten anything through the two rounds of security."

He leaned back. "I find myself a bit more careful these days."

"These days?"

"Since your brother stole from me then turned around a few days later and tried to throw the scent off him by taking public shots at me." Derrick motioned toward the chair next to her.

"So, that's it. The rumors, the photos, the fake social news suggesting we're together." She dumped her purse on the seat but remained on her feet. "You're coming after me to get even. This is some sort of weird revenge."

Derrick nodded. "A fascinating theory."

That really was the only explanation. Even though money had always been tight, Noah wasn't the type to steal.

"I see the dramatic streak runs in the family." Derrick's exhale filled the room. "Lucky me."

Right. I'm the dramatic one. "Says the guy who has a private butler and an office set off from everyone else."

"Security."

Everything inside her froze. "Excuse me?"

"Jackson is my head of security."

She relaxed but not much. Something told her she needed to be on her toes with this guy. He might talk smooth and look like he stepped out of her hottest fantasy, but that didn't change the facts. He was a ruthless jackass. "Do that many people want to kill you?"

"My family has significant business interests. That sort of thing tends to attract trouble."

She'd never been called that before. "Are you referring to me as the trouble?"

He shrugged. "Let's hope not."

She'd taken about all of the put-her-on-the-defensive moves that she could stand. It was time to get to the point so she could run out of there. "Mr. Jame—"

"I believe I asked you to call me Derrick."

That's what she called him in her head… "Do you think that's wise?"

"I'm afraid you've lost me."

"You and my brother are locked in some sort of public pissing match. You're threatening him with lawyers. He's making you look bad on the internet, which has bled over to traditional media." She put her palms on his desk and leaned in. "What I'm saying is that fake rumors or not, we're on opposite sides of this battle."

His gaze skimmed over her. "We don't have to be."

He hadn't moved but the heated words swept over her in a caress that had her shaking her head and standing straight again. She not only needed to be careful with Derrick, she needed body armor.

She blocked out every other thought and concentrated on the guy she'd come to think of as cold-blooded. "Has anyone ever pointed out your cryptic way of speaking?"

"Then let me be clear." Derrick balanced his elbows on the edge of his desk and leaned in toward her. "Your brother took money out of my business accounts and is going to go to jail unless I step in and save him."

"No, that's not—"

Derrick held up a finger. "There's nothing to debate. That's a fact." He let his hand fall again. "But I am willing to help him."

She could almost feel a trap closing over her head. The need to bolt overtook her but she forced her legs to stay still. "Why?"

"Most people would ask how."

She refused to be taken off guard by double-talk. "I'm not like everyone else."

"I'm starting to see that." Derrick watched her for a second. His gaze moved over her face in the silence. After a visible inhale, he began again, his voice louder and more firm. "I will help your brother but he has to do something for me."

"You don't like that he's making you look like a complete jerk, maybe even a bit incompetent." She got that.

Derrick fired Noah eight weeks ago, exactly two weeks before she lost her job. Noah's videos started out as a way to let off steam. Then he gained followers. A lot of them. He even managed to make money off his internet work, but she had no idea how.

He'd become a symbol for the "little man" fighting against the corporate machine. As his following grew, so did his stories about Derrick and the company.

Blame it on Noah's baby face or his sarcasm, but media and online sites had picked up the battle. Then Derrick's lawyers had made contact…and so had the prosecutor's office about the missing funds.

And now Derrick had the *Insider* and its gossip network working for him.

"I have shareholders and business associates," Derrick said.

"So, this is about money."

Derrick's frown deepened. "Isn't everything?"

Not an unexpected answer, but still… "It worries me that you don't know how scary that question is."

"I'm proposing a quid pro quo. I make your brother's legal issues disappear. He shuts down his site and I assist him in finding other more profitable and appropriate ways to channel his technology experience."

That sounded somewhat reasonable, which scared her. "That's the entire deal you're offering?"

"No."

She beat back a wave of disappointment. She'd taken care of her brilliant brother for so long. Tried to keep him occupied and out of trouble. The idea of having someone else handle that job sounded really good to her at the moment. With her life in shambles and the need to find a new job nipping at her, she loved the idea of having one less stress to deal with.

"I haven't told you what I get out of this," Derrick said.

Her heart sank. She held in a groan before it could escape her lips. "You did. He stops running the site."

It might sound easy but it wasn't. Noah didn't have anything else right now except for his anger at Derrick and the attention from his videos. It was the "thing" that kept Noah going. It also provided him with more attention and praise than he'd ever gotten.

"The damage is done. He's lied and caused me what could be irreparable damage," Derrick said.

His words pounded her but she kept her shoulders up and her back straight. "That sounds like a legal term."

"Because it is."

That meant more fighting. More lawyer fees on top of the ones for her employment attorney. "I thought you were worried about the lost money."

"There are bigger issues here."

She couldn't imagine money being a side concern. "Noah is a kid."

"Noah is twenty and a genius." When she opened her mouth to respond, Derrick talked right over her. "You are twenty-nine, which means you're old enough to know he's looking at criminal charges and civil repercussions for the money, which I'm willing to overlook right now."

"I'm going to pretend I know what that means and jump ahead. What is your part of the quid pro quo? Because you don't strike me as a guy who does things to be nice." That wasn't quite true. He'd hired Noah and ignored his lack of a degree and questionable people skills. But he'd also had security escort Noah out of the building months later. Now that she knew how that felt, she had even more sympathy for her brother. "What do you want?"

"You."

A weird, high-pitched ringing filled her ears. She shook her head but it refused to die down. "What?"

"The carefully placed stories about us have been aimed at diffusing some of your brother's damage."

"In other words, you're using me to somehow make yourself look better."

He shrugged. "That's not the way I'd put it."

"Of course not, since you're clearly clueless about women."

That had him sitting straighter. "Excuse me?"

Bull's-eye. The idea that she'd found the one thing sure to grab his attention—questioning his success with women—filled her with relief. "You're letting people believe we're together and—"

"Dating. People are starting to believe we're dating and that your brother doesn't like it and is trying to break us up by launching false charges against me." Derrick looked far too pleased with himself. "Which was exactly my plan."

"That's ridiculous." She could think of a lot of other words to describe it but kept the conversation G-rated.

"I thought so, too, when the PR team suggested it, but I guess the public does like a good love story."

A scream rattled around inside her. "Did you ever think to ask me first?"

"No."

The quick response had her sputtering. "That's really your answer?"

"I called you *lovely* in my interview with the *Insider*, which I think we can agree was a bit of a stretch since you looked ready to punch me the first time we met in person."

"Oh, you picked up on that?" *Good to know.*

"Let's get down to it." He leaned in again. Didn't break eye contact. "We're talking about a business arrangement."

"Who is?"

"You will pose as my girlfriend for an appropriate length of time, short though because the timing is important here. Long enough for us to sell that we've been dating. Then you'll act as my fiancée and—"

"Wait." That ringing in her ears turned into a loud clanging sound.

He stared at her. "I haven't finished explaining the plan."

When his PR team said he'd needed to create a diversion, it made sense in an abstract sort of way. But they could not have meant her. He—they—didn't even know her. And no way did they mean an engagement.

She suspected they'd talked about him finding a life outside the office. She tried to direct him there. "I'm sure there are women in town who would want to date you. It's tough out there and my brother isn't exactly highlighting your good side. But you have money and you're…you know…"

He studied her now, like how he might study something on the bottom of his shoe. "I have no idea what you're trying to say."

"Well, your face is…fine." As in perfect and compelling. Way too kissable.

His eyes widened. *"Fine?"*

Because space seemed like a good idea she stepped away from the desk. Tried to draw enough air into her lungs and head to be able to breathe again. "Don't rich people travel in packs? I'm sure you can hang out at your country club or polo club, or wherever it is you go for fun, and find a nice woman who—"

"I am not hard up for a date." He sounded stunned at the idea.

"Well, there." She almost clapped but decided that was too much. "Good for you."

"I am, however, on the wrong side of your brother's ill-advised rant." He made a face that suggested he thought she should be picking up on his point a bit faster. "I explained this to you at the hotel."

"You said you needed good news to balance out the bad." That made sense, which only made her wariness tick up even higher. "So, hire someone to pretend date you if you don't want an actual girlfriend."

"It needs to be you. You provide a reason for your brother's specific attack." When she tried to stop him, he kept right on talking. Rolled right over her. "We put on a very public show. We get people to see us as a couple, get engaged—not for real, of course—and we neutralize some of the damage your brother has done."

"A fake fiancée." She said the words nice and slow, thinking he'd stop her because he had to be kidding.

Never mind that she could barely stand him. Sure, she'd spun wild daydreams about him. Even imagined what he might look like without that serious suit and the fancy office, but come on.

"Exactly." The phone on his desk rang. He hit a button and the sound cut off. "You've spent a significant part of your life protecting your baby brother and I suspect you will continue to do so now, even though it's misguided."

That hit a bit too close to the comments Vanessa had made last night. "Misguided? I'm confused. Are you arguing for this fake engagement thing or not?"

"People will see us together, which will telegraph the message that I am not the man your brother says I am. You wouldn't date me otherwise. It will be a business arrangement that will benefit you greatly, and it will keep me from going after him for the money." He shrugged. "And, since time is a factor, I went ahead and started the rumors. As you know."

"Because that made sense to you?"

"Because your brother is in serious legal trouble and I can help him. I can also provide some guidance for the future and take the pressure off you. In many ways."

For the first time she noticed his hands. Those long fingers. The strength. The way he rubbed his palms together as if that in-control voice didn't quite match whatever was happening inside him.

But none of that calmed her wariness. Not when every word he uttered carried a note of a threat. "What does that mean?"

"You were recently fired."

Her stomach dropped, and not in a good way. Forget his deep, soothing voice and the sexy confidence that thrummed off him. If he made one wrong comment about her losing her job she would lunge across the desk and strangle him with that blue tie. "Laid off."

"We both know that's not true." Derrick didn't stop talking long enough to let her break in. "It would appear I'm not the only one who has an image to salvage. While you're doing that, I will pay your bills."

That sounded like…well, not good. "No."

"Consider this an acting role of sorts. One for which you should be paid." He picked up the folder in front of him and slid it toward her. "Here."

"What's that?"

"A contract."

The guy was prepared. She had to give him that. "You think I'm going to say yes then sign something?"

"Why wouldn't you?"

"Love, honor, decency." She probably should have thrown in a few more words but her brain refused to reboot. It had been misfiring ever since he'd smiled that first time.

"I'm not sure what any of those have to do with this arrangement." He nodded at the folder. "Take a look. Everyone benefits."

"Mostly you."

"I don't deny I get something out of this, but so do you. More important, so does Noah."

That sounded good but she doubted Derrick would deal fairly with Noah at this point. She couldn't believe the charges against her brother. But the idea that Derrick would waste time going after Noah if he was innocent didn't make much sense, either.

As soon as the doubts crept into her head about her brother, she tried to push them out again. *Be loyal.* "Noah denies the charges."

"He's lying." Derrick didn't even flinch as he talked. Never broke eye contact. Didn't give away any sign that he doubted what he said.

Something about his coolness made her insides shake. "Why should I believe you over my brother?"

"Deep down, you know I'm right."

"I don't think—"

"Yes, it would be better if you didn't, but I'm betting you will study this proposal from every angle." Derrick put his hand on the folder. "You can have until tomorrow morning."

She had to grab on to the chair next to her for balance. The room had started spinning and with each word he said rocked her harder. "For what?"

"To give me your response. As I said, time is of the essence. I am currently holding off the prosecutor but he needs an answer about your brother."

"And he'll do what you say?"

"We went to college together."

"Of course you did." From her experience with the job search she knew powerful people stuck together. But the caress of Derrick's voice, the concern in his tone—it all had her taking another step back. "This bargain or offer or whatever it is…it's ridiculous. You know that, right? I need to know you know that."

But even as she said the words her mind starting working. He could help Noah. She could get her life in order. Derrick offered breathing room and support, and that tempted her even though she knew she couldn't trust him one inch.

"Your brother's actions leave me with little option, and he shows no signs of stopping even if he is arrested. Shareholder discontent is an issue. I also have a reputation in the community."

"One that would suffer if people found out you made an offer for a fake fiancée."

He hadn't been moving but still his body froze. "Is that a threat, Ellie?"

"I'm trying to understand why a man with your money and power would make this offer."

"That's my problem, not yours."

"If I'm going to be your fiancée then—"

He held up a hand. "In name only."

"No sex then?" *Where had that come from*?

His eyebrow lifted. "I am willing to negotiate that point. Very willing."

She could almost feel his fingertips brush over her. "Forget it."

"You have until tomorrow at ten to give me an answer." He broke eye contact and hit a button on his phone. "Not ten after, Ellie. Ten exactly."

It was a dismissal. She heard it, felt it and ignored it. "I wouldn't clear your calendar if I were you."

He didn't look up. "Ten."

Three

Derrick leaned back in his oversize desk chair and blew out a long, haggard breath as the door closed behind Ellie and she left his office. He'd expected anger and a hint of distrust. He would have worried if she'd said yes to his fake engagement offer and jumped in. Eagerness was not a bonus in this type of situation.

No, he'd been prepared for all that. The sucker punch of need that slammed in to his gut the second he saw her again? That one had been a surprise.

She'd walked in with her long brown hair tied up behind her head with those strands hanging down, all sexy and loose. She'd worn a thin black skirt and white shirt and all he could think about was stripping both off her. The tight body. Those legs. The way fire lit her hazel eyes as she argued.

It all worked for him.

His attraction to her had sparked the minute she'd opened her mouth. She was tough and smart, and not easy to throw off or to scare. She met every one of his verbal shots with one of her own.

The woman was hot, no question.

She didn't fit his usual type.

He thought about the women he'd dated over the past few years. All cool, reserved business types. He preferred competent over sparks and heat. Maybe that's why the last three were now some of this favorite business associates. Friends, even.

He didn't believe in the idea of grand love. That struck him as nonsense. He'd grown up in a family that yelled. His father pitted him and his two brothers against each other. At his urging, they'd been racing and competing since the cradle. Every mistake had been dissected and fed back to them in an endless loop by their unforgiving father and then by the press that followed the Jameson boys' every move.

Never mind that Derrick's grandfather was a disgraced congressman or that their father, Eldrick Jameson, a self-made man with three former wives and a new much-younger one, had made his initial millions, before he lost them, by not always playing fair. Derrick and his brothers were magazine and news favorites, and few in the press gave them favorable coverage no matter what they did.

No, Derrick didn't believe much in emotions. But he did believe in this company. He'd rebuilt it from the dust left over from his father's fires and while the old man ran through woman after woman. Derrick labored over every contract and every deal. Gave his life to it. And now he was getting screwed by the old man—again.

His father handed down his requirements for turning the business over, the main one being that Derrick clean up his reputation and resolve "the Noah problem" within ninety days. That meant dealing with Ellie since his PR team thought trying to deal with Noah directly could result in another video.

From the photos he'd seen of her before they met at the party, he'd expected pretty in a girl-next-door kind of way. Quiet. Not someone likely to light his fire. From what he knew about her job situation, he'd expected desperation and a willingness to deal.

He got none of that.

Jackson Richards opened the door and slid inside the office. He wore a stupid grin as he walked across the office and stopped in front of Derrick. "She's not what I expected."

Now there was an understatement. "Me, either. And did you call me *sir* earlier?" That was new and Derrick didn't like it.

Jackson shrugged. "I thought it fit with the mood you were trying to create."

"You can skip the overly deferential act. I have enough people around here who do that."

"Are you engaged yet?" Jackson sounded amused at the idea.

Derrick was happy someone thought the nightmare situation was funny. "She's difficult."

"She sounds perfect for you."

Jackson was one of the few people who could get away with the comment. They'd known each other for years and were about the same age, both in their midthirties. Eldrick had brought Jackson into the company, but Derrick liked him despite that. They'd been friends from the start. With Jackson, Derrick let the firm line between boss and employee blur.

But right now his mind was on the hot brunette with the impressive ass who'd just left his office. "She seems to think I should be able to find a real date."

"Did you tell her about your father's conditions for signing the business over to you and how you have something of an impossible deadline in which to meet them?"

The damn agreement. Leave it to Eldrick to make everything difficult. "You mean selling it to me? For a lot of money he can then spend on my new stepmother? Of course not."

Jackson winced. "It might help your case."

"I doubt Ellie would be sympathetic."

"Not if you keep placing false rumors with the *Insider*." Jackson shook his head. "I warned you that could backfire. Women hate stuff like that, and with good reason."

"Speaking of which, is the photographer waiting outside?" That's why her tardiness mattered. Much later and she would have blown his plans.

"When Ellie figures out you staged this meeting to get a photo of her coming out of your office she's—"

"Going to yell." Derrick knew it. He even felt a twinge of guilt over it—one he could easily ignore. "But we know this is about more than a PR job. This is about saving the company and there's no way I'm letting her know I need her help for something that big. I'm not giving her that power over me."

"Very romantic."

"This is business. According to my father's stipulations, I have to get my brothers in line and in this office, clean up my image and stop Noah Gold's public hit job, all while single-handedly running a commercial real estate company."

After a lifetime of aiming his sons at each other, Derrick's father wanted them to be one big happy family, all working in the office and getting along. And if they didn't, Derrick would lose the business that meant everything to him. His father already had a buyer outside the family interested. A rich old friend with liquidity and the ability to move fast on the sale.

Just thinking about the requirements of his father's stupid business proposal touched off a new wave of fury in Derrick's gut. He literally could forfeit everything because of his father's stupid whims.

Derrick was about to launch into an angry rant about Eldrick when his office door pushed open. Ellie stepped inside again, looking a little flushed and not a bit worried or afraid of him.

He liked her attitude but the security lapse was a concern. Then he thought about the photographer and wondered if the guy had moved too soon. "How did you get in here?"

"I walked."

He guessed he should have expected that answer from her. "You shouldn't be able to wander around the building without an escort."

She waved the concern away as she approached the desk and held out her hand. "You can worry about your over-the-top paranoid protocol later. Give me the agreement."

"What?"

She continued to hold out her hand. "If I'm going to consider this—"

"Are you?" That surprised him when almost nothing did.

"—I want to make sure you didn't add anything weird in here."

Whatever he planned to say left his head. He suddenly wanted to know what her definition of "weird" might be. "Like what?"

"With you?" She snorted. "Who knows? I don't trust you."

Jackson nodded as he grabbed the folder and gave it to her. "A very solid beginning for a relationship."

Her eyes narrowed as her gaze moved from Jackson to Derrick. "Your guy knows about this nonsense fake dating and engagement offer of yours?"

"Yes, and that document in your hand is nonnegotiable." Derrick knew from their combined thirty minutes together so far that she'd be whipping out the red pen and revising if he didn't put a stop to it now.

She shrugged at him as she opened the file and took a peek inside. "Whatever."

He fought back a sigh. "I'm serious, Ellie."

Her head shot up and she glared at him. "You're not going to win every argument."

"I think I am." He rarely lost and had no intention of starting now. "I'll see you at ten tomorrow."

She turned and headed for the door. "You'll get my answer when you get it."

She was gone before Derrick could respond.

Damn, he liked her. The fire and self-assurance were so sexy. She wasn't yet thirty but she'd grown up fast when she'd lost her parents. He understood what it was like to take on responsibility early. It was one of the reasons he thought they'd be able to handle this arrangement. She would get what she needed and he'd get his obstinate father off his back.

Jackson cleared his throat. "You're smiling."

Derrick refused to play this game. "She's…interesting."

"This engagement thing *is* fake, right?"

"Of course."

"Right." Jackson exhaled. "That explains the stupid look on your face whenever you see her."

Four

The DC Insider: *Visits to the prestigious Hay-Adams. Visits to his office. It appears Ms. Ellie Gold has not only snagged our Hottest Ticket in Town's attention but also has him spinning in circles. Well done, Ellie!*

He had to be kidding. That thought kept running through Ellie's mind as she paged through Derrick's ten—no, fourteen-page agreement while sitting on her couch the next morning.

The thing had tiny print, and rules, and footnotes to new rules and references to yet more rules. The list of restrictions seemed endless. She couldn't date anyone else. He had final approval over the people she saw on a friendly basis during the "term of their arrangement" and over any work plans she intended to pursue.

She had to act loving, whatever that meant. He hadn't used the word *obey* but it was implied in almost every line. And that wasn't even the most ridiculous part. He thought they'd live together. *Actually live together.*

She glanced around her small apartment, from one stack of empty boxes to another. She had savings but that would run out if she didn't find a new job and a cheaper place to live soon. That would be easier if her jackass of an ex-boss hadn't launched an offensive strike when she filed her internal complaint and fired her first, insisting she came on to him. As if that would ever happen.

The man's wife had left town to watch over a sick aunt and he'd had his hands all over her by the next day. Kicking him in the crotch had felt great, but being escorted out of the building hadn't.

His claims were nonsense. He had resources and family money…and a nasty reputation that people spoke about only in whispers and refused to confirm in public. She had documentation of the emails she'd sent after the incident and her complaint. No witnesses to what happened, unfortunately, but she guessed they'd be able to find a pattern of other women once they started digging.

Her lawyer was positive about her chances but cases cost money. She got that but employers weren't exactly lining up to hire a supposed human resources expert who had been fired for making a play for her boss. She could not let this go. Not when it was likely he would do this to someone else.

Thinking about Joe touched off that familiar spiraling sensation in her stomach. That mix of panic and worry. She liked to eat and have electricity. Which led her to the convoluted mess of an agreement on her lap.

Derrick's plan struck her as so odd. She had no idea if wealthy people usually did stuff like this, but she didn't.

She picked up her mug of now-cool tea and prepared to read through the agreement one more time. The doorbell stopped her in the middle of what looked like a never-ending sentence of legalese gobbledygook.

Grumbling, she put down the mug and stood. Slipping her feet into her fluffy pink slippers, she shuffled across the floor. That took about ten seconds since she lived in a studio.

When the doorbell rang again, she skipped her usual check in the mirror by the door. Anyone this impatient deserved to be greeted with the full hair-sliding-out-of-the-ponytail style she had going on.

She peeked through the peephole and froze. *Oh, no, no, no.*

He was here. Now. At her house.

"Open up, Ellie." Derrick's deep voice floated through the door.

She tried not to make a sound.

He sighed loud enough to shake the building. "I can see your shadow under the door."

"Fine." She performed the perfect eye roll as she undid the lock. "What?"

He started talking before she fully opened the door. "It's eleven."

"I own a clock." Though she guessed she looked as if she didn't own a brush. She could practically feel the tangles in her hair without touching it. Add in the shorts and oversize sweater that functioned as her pajamas and she was positive she made quite the picture.

"Are you sure?" His gaze wandered over her and stopped on her slippers. "Those are an unexpected choice."

"Imagine me kicking you with them." She stepped to the side and let him in. Why fight it? He was not exactly the type to scamper off.

He slipped past her, smelling all fresh and clean. Today's suit was navy blue and fit him, slid over every inch of him, perfectly.

He walked to the center of the room then turned around to face her. "You were supposed to be in my office at ten."

No doubt about it, he was much hotter when he didn't talk. "No, you commanded that I give you an answer to your absurd fake engagement suggestion by a stated time and I declined."

"Interesting."

Since that could refer to anything, she ignored it and focused on another annoying fact. "Hey, how did you know where I live?"

He shot her a look that suggested he found the question ridiculous. "Please."

That was not even a little reassuring. "Did Jackson follow me?"

"Jackson is in the car."

Okay... "Is that an answer?"

Derrick looked around the room, from the couch to the rows of bookcases lining the walls and holding her collection of romances and mysteries. He kept going, skipping over the kitchenette and falling on the unmade bed against the far wall.

He turned and stared at her again, his expression blank. "Yes or no, Ellie."

She didn't pretend to misunderstand. He was talking about the agreement. He needed a fake fiancée and, for whatever reason, thought she fit the description. "It's not that simple."

"It actually is."

Of course he would think so. The entire agreement benefitted him. "We don't know each other."

He frowned. "You said that already. So?"

Such a guy. "Really? That's your answer?"

"Again, for what feels like the tenth time, this is a business arrangement, not an actual romance."

She joined him by the couch. "Now you sound ticked off."

"I hate repetition."

Poor baby. "Do you want a fiancée or not? Because I would be doing this for you, not me."

"We both know that's not true. You benefit. Your brother benefits." Derrick shifted his weight and looked down. He stared at the magazines piled on her floor for a few seconds then pushed them to the side with his foot. "All you need to do is follow a few simple rules."

She didn't bother to debate his idea of a "few" because that could take them all day. From his scowl she guessed he wanted to add another provision to the agreement to forbid her slight tendency toward clutter.

"You say that but everyone I know needs to believe it's real." She scooped up the agreement and flipped through the pages then began pointing. "Here, look at this."

He didn't bother to glance down. "I'm familiar with the contract."

"Then you know we're supposed to live together." Which sounded as absurd this time as when she'd read it earlier.

"My house is big." His gaze wandered again. This time over to the boxes she'd gathered in case she needed to move in a hurry. "But I prefer you not live out of boxes. Haven't you been in this apartment for seven months, like right before Noah started working for me?"

She snapped her fingers. "Derrick."

"Don't do that. Ever." He put his hand over hers and lowered it. "What do you want to say?"

The touch, so simple and innocent, shot through her. She felt it vibrate through every cell.

She pulled her hand from his and forced her breathing to slow. "We've barely spent an hour together."

"We'll have separate bedrooms."

As if that were the only problem. "But you expect me to act like a fiancée."

"Whatever that means, yes."

"It's a direct quote from paragraph twenty of this thing." She shook the agreement at him.

"I've never been engaged, but I figure we can work out the details as we go. You know, like do the usual things engaged people do."

She suddenly couldn't breathe. A big lump clogged her throat and she had no idea why. "Usual?"

"Shows of…affection."

He may as well have said poison. "You should hear yourself."

He exhaled as he stepped back. His hand swept

through his hair and, for a brief moment, his thick wall of confidence slipped. He looked vulnerable and frustrated. She didn't think any of it was aimed at her. Not directly. This was more about the circumstances they'd gotten stuck in.

"We both need things, Ellie. You want to help your brother. You have some work issues that I can resolve for you."

"Are you going to give me a job?" She thought about her bills and her fears about losing her apartment. Growing up she never felt welcome or comfortable. Home hadn't been a sanctuary, but now it was. The idea she could lose that security left her shaken.

"Yes, as my fiancée."

With him that *did* sound like a full-time job. But pretending to have feelings might not be enough. They didn't run in the same circles. She didn't know anything about charity functions or season tickets to the Kennedy Center. "People aren't going to buy this."

He stepped closer again. This time CEO his hands came up and his palms rubbed up and down her arms, gentle and warm. "We tell them we met while haggling about your brother. There was a spark and…boom."

"Did you just say *boom*?"

Instead of backing away, he leaned in. "The legal fees stop. Your brother gets some direction and guidance. Your bills get paid and my shareholders stop whining."

"You make it sound reasonable in a weird sort of way." She was practical and everything about this plan, including the very real problem of lying to her brother, was anything but.

"It is."

"My brother will go ballistic." And she feared that was an understatement.

"Trust me. We can sell this."

She didn't miss the fact his words sounded like a plea. She doubted he begged for anything. He probably didn't even ask others for help, but he was asking now.

The realization had her stomach tumbling. This close she could see the intensity in his gaze and feel the heat rolling off him.

"You can't fake a spark." Her voice sounded breathy even in her ears.

"Let's see if we need to."

He lowered his head as his hand slid into her hair. Fingers expertly massaged the back of her neck. His mouth lowered until it hovered over hers. For a second he hesitated, with his eyes searching her face, then his lips met hers. Mouth against mouth, he brushed over hers once. Twice. So enticing.

His scent wrapped around her and his fingers tightened on her. One second they stood a foot apart. The next he closed in. The caress turned to kissing, deep and alive with need. Energy arced between them. Every touch, every press of his lips, proved hot and inviting.

He pulled her tight against him and her common sense faltered. Heat burned through her as her arms slipped up to wrap around his neck. She'd just balanced against his body when he pulled back.

"Right." He cleared his throat as his chest rose and fell on harsh breaths. "There we go."

A haze covered her brain. *"There we go?"*

"Sure. That was fine." He set her away from him. Increased the distance between them to a few feet.

The man was an idiot.

"Fine?" She could barely feel her legs.

"Yes. I'm confident we can fake it." He started walking around the room, almost pacing. "We'll start with dates. In public. Let people see us together." He nodded as he continued the one-sided conversation. "I'd say in a week we move you into my place and announce the engagement."

"That's too fast." She was impressed her brain even spit that sentence out. Right now she couldn't think at all. The kiss had blown out every rational thought and had her wanting to slide that tie right off him.

"Well, it looks as if you're ready to pack."

"I need to sit." She plunked down hard on the armrest of the couch and struggled not to run her fingertips over her lips.

"We'll have a party—"

"No." Good grief, he was already planning. That was enough to snap her out of it.

"Not a big, flashy Christmas party. Just the normal engagement party."

It took a few seconds but her common sense came back. Doubt rushed in right behind it.

"First, it's March. Second, I'm Jewish." That seemed important to throw in there even in a fake engagement, so she did. "And third... I fear your idea of normal."

"We invite the people who need to see us."

People who would later wonder what happened and why it all ended, but he seemed to ignore that part. Fine. It was his problem and they were his friends, so he could figure it out. But she did have one issue she could not ignore. "And what do I tell my brother to keep him from killing you?"

"That we sparked. Tell him a one-night stand turned into something more."

Derrick. Sex. She blocked the thoughts that rolled through her head. The kiss had been enough to un-ravel her. Anything more would be a huge mistake. "You want me to lie to him?"

"That's the point. We lie to him and the public to diffuse Noah's claims."

She couldn't blame Derrick for that requirement. Noah hadn't exactly been subtle in his attack on Der-rick to date. But something about his self-assurance about this agreement and all these details started an alarm bell ringing in her head. "You have this all fig-ured out, don't you?"

"I thought so."

She swung her foot, letting the pink slipper flip through the air. "What does that mean?"

"You're not what I expected."

She stilled. "Right back at ya."

"Lucky for us, I can adapt."

Yeah, lucky her. "You don't exactly strike me as a guy who enjoys surprises."

Some of the tension drained from his face as he stared at her. That sexy little smile of his returned. "Maybe I can change."

She hadn't known that to work with any guy ever. "Oh, come on."

He walked up to her and picked the agreement off her lap. "Sign."

"You know you can't date anyone else while we're pretending to like each other, right?" For some reason it was suddenly very important to her that he know if she did this, they did it together. They'd both suffer.

He made a face. "Does it say that?"

"It will when we write in a bunch of notes in the margin and both initial them." She tapped the agreement. "Basically, every ridiculous provision that applies to me will now apply to you."

He didn't hesitate. "Fine."

That was almost too easy. "That means you're stuck with me for... Wait, there's no end time on this agreement."

His eyebrow lifted. "I'm aware."

For about the hundredth time since she'd met him yesterday she got the sense she was being outmaneuvered. She hated the sensation. "You get two months of fake fiancée time."

"That might not be enough. Say at least three."

She reached down and picked a pen up off her coffee table. She clicked the end and handed it to him. "I'm sure you can adapt to two."

"It seems you think I'll be adapting a lot over the next few weeks." He sounded stunned by the idea.

"I'm happy you realize that. It will make our time together, limited though it may be, more tolerable."

His smile widened. "We'll see."

Five

The DC Insider: *We are hearing that our Hottest Ticket in Town wants to get serious with his new lady but the lady's disgruntled baby brother is having none of it. He's making some big claims, all of which Derrick Jameson denies with a shrug. But can this budding romance bloom with all these distractions?*

Ellie was starting to think her headache would never go away. It thumped in her ears and over her eyes. Even the back of her neck ached.

She'd had two employment interviews today and nothing. Well, not nothing. In the second, the interviewer wanted to talk about Derrick. He didn't specifically ask about her dating life but he bounced around the topic, honing in on her "influence" over Derrick and his decisions and questioning if that would be a conflict. Since she was trying for a generalist HR position—one unrelated to Derrick or his habit of buying up most of the property in the city—she couldn't imagine what Derrick had to do with her possible paycheck.

Being a fake fiancée had sounded easy, two months of playtime while they went to dinner and she didn't panic about the water bill, but it was starting to take over her life. In addition to thinking about him and that voice…and that face…she had other issues. She'd splurged on a muffin at the coffee place around the corner that morning and two people took her photo.

And then there was the *Insider*. Her teeth ground together at the idea of being in the *Insider*'s daily round-up section for two more months. Derrick needed to knock that off. She knew she should have insisted on a "no talking to gossip sites" clause in that stupid agreement. But she hadn't, so now she nursed a glass of wine as she propped her feet on her coffee table and tried to pretend she was stuck in a bad dream.

She'd managed to kick her heels off and find her pink slippers. She had no idea where she'd thrown her suit jacket. Since she couldn't afford new clothes or a big dry-cleaning bill right now, not when she was saving every penny just in case, that could be a problem. She'd just leaned her head against the couch cushion when she heard the rattling. She stared at the ceiling for a second, trying to place the sound.

Jingling. Keys.

The mix of sounds had her jackknifing and jumping to her feet. The wine went *everywhere*. Down her shirt. On her couch. A line ran over her hand as more dripped onto the carpet, destroying any chance of getting that security deposit she so desperately needed back.

The door opened and she spun around, ready to throw the glass. She stopped just in time.

The wind rushed out of her. "Noah?"

Her brother stood there with a face flushed red with fury and his hands balled into fists at his sides. He looked ready to launch. She stepped back without thinking and rammed her calf into the edge of the coffee table.

"What are you thinking?" He hovered in the doorway, with the open hallway to her neighbors in the three-story, converted apartment building right there.

That tone, deep and shaking, brought back memories of the days before she'd found the right doctor for him. Once she'd understood that her parents had caused more trouble for him by not immediately seeking treatment and that the delay could lead to bigger issues later in life, she got Noah help.

But that didn't solve the problem completely. Even now, the more stressed, the more under fire he felt, the more skewed his boundaries became. The uncontrolled anger of the past when he would punch walls was gone, but the faint whisper of frustration remained.

Disregarding the way her shirt now stuck to her skin and the wet chilling her from the inside out, she inhaled and pitched her voice low. "Are you okay? It's not like you to barge in."

"I thought you might have someone in here and not let me open up," he said.

That struck her as the worst response ever. She set

her now-empty glass on a months-old magazine and stared him down. "And you thought that entitled you to use the emergency key?"

"Do you really care that I came in without knocking?"

That was a typical Noah response. He flipped things around to make her feel like the unreasonable one. "It's a matter of privacy."

"I want an explanation." He stepped into the apartment, leaving the door hanging open behind him.

"You mean Derrick." At the use of the name, she could see Noah's jaw clench. His features hardened.

With the straight brown hair and dark brown eyes, Noah looked like their father. While Dad's perpetual good looks and boyish charm had helped to launch him in hundreds of get-rich-schemes over the years, including the one her parents were flying to when they died, Noah tended to be aloof and always assessing.

He came around to the same side of the couch as her. "You're on a first-name basis with the guy who fired me and is trying to frame me?"

She wasn't sure how to broach this subject but she tried anyway… "Is it possible this thing between the two of you has gone off the tracks a bit?" When Noah's mouth dropped open, she hurried to finish the thought. "Maybe there was a miscommunication and then you—"

"He's brainwashed you." Noah sounded stunned at the idea.

She tried to ignore how insulting that was. Tried and couldn't. "What?"

"Is it the money?"

And he made it worse. "What are you talking about?"

"Look, I know you've had a tough time dating and stuff, but Derrick Jameson?" Noah asked. "People are asking me about you and Jameson in the comment sections of my videos. They're questioning *me* now."

So that was it. His precious videos. His crusade. Just once she wished someone would care about her. "That's what this is about? I'm messing up your revenge plans?"

"Having my sister sleep with my enemy is a problem, yes." Noah practically spat as he talked and stepped toward her.

Out of habit, she moved back. He wouldn't hurt her, but he sometimes still funneled his frustration into throwing things, and she did not want to be in the firing line. "You sound like you're twelve."

"He really does."

A now-familiar deep voice sounded from the doorway. Relief slammed into Ellie before she even looked over. It washed right through her, calming her down.

Derrick. He loomed there, wearing a dark suit and fierce frown. The glare did not waver away from Noah.

"You're here." Noah's shoulders fell as if a load of shock had replaced his anger. "In my sister's house."

"You always were very observant." Derrick stepped inside and closed the door behind him.

The soft thud snapped Ellie out of the haze enveloping her. That fast, she flipped from soothing mode to trying to wrestle control back. "Derrick, sarcasm is not helping here."

He looked at her then. His gaze traveled over her, hesitating on the stain plastering her silk blouse to her chest before bouncing up again. "Sorry."

The word sounded so sincere and heartfelt. As if he understood she was ten seconds away from shattering into a million pieces.

"You apologized to her?" Noah's full attention centered on Derrick. "What about me?"

"You stole from me and got caught." Derrick's voice stayed steady even as he shook his head. "If you needed money you could have asked for an advance on your salary." Derrick's eyes narrowed. "But I'm not sure any of this was about money."

Noah turned to face her again. "Do you hear him? His accusations?"

She did. Saw him, too. Watching Derrick was a revelation. If he carried around any guilt, he hid it well. If he had falsely blamed Noah...no, that didn't make sense. It had never made sense, but seeing Derrick now, in full de-escalation mode, made her brother's story even less believable.

She inhaled, trying to calm the last of her frayed nerves, and pointed toward the now wine-stained couch. "Maybe we could all sit down."

"Not with him." Noah pushed by Derrick. Shoved his shoulder into him and kept going. Didn't say anything until he reached the door. "Just wait until the next video."

As soon as Noah's hand hit the doorknob, Derrick spoke up. "Post whatever you want about me but keep your sister out of it."

Noah slowly turned around to face Derrick. "You think you get to order me around when I'm not working for you?"

"If you have a problem, you come for me." He pointed toward Ellie. "Not her. Not ever."

Noah's face went blank. "She's my sister."

"Then act like it."

Derrick forced himself not to follow Noah out the door. He wanted to have it out, make the kid understand he was playing in an adult world now.

Instead he stood there, staring at the door and trying to ease his temper. Something had happened before he'd walked down that hallway and heard the shouting. Ellie was drenched in wine. Hell, it beaded in her hair. But nothing, no furniture or glass, appeared to be broken.

She shook her head. "So much for thinking I was going to be able to enjoy two months of fake engagement bliss."

"Did I promise that?"

"Honestly, no. But I knew my brother would be a bigger problem than you thought." Ellie said the words on a heavy sigh.

Derrick looked at her again. "Your brother is—"

"Still my brother, so be careful with what words you use."

That seemed like the Ellie he'd experienced so far—tough and sure—but the tone sounded defeated. He hated that. "Right."

"He's upset." She lifted the wineglass from the coffee table and a magazine page stuck to it.

"Yeah, I picked up on that."

"He was diagnosed years ago with this disorder you've likely never heard of. Believe it or not, this is a thousand times better than he used to be." She held the glass in midair, peeling the paper off with a loud ripping sound. "His teen years were exhausting."

That was enough of that. Derrick stepped over to her and put his hand over hers. With one quick tug, he liberated the glass then carried it to her kitchen sink. "He's not a teen now, so don't make excuses for him."

"I'm explaining that this is not a matter of him being spoiled."

"Are you willing to concede that, maybe, you make it easy for him to not deal with his issues as an adult?" He stopped for a second with his hands wrapped around the edge of the counter.

Noah was nothing like Derrick's father, Eldrick, except that people rushed to forgive both of them. That innate ability to have people fall all over themselves trying to make things rights and ease any burden... Derrick didn't get it. No one had ever done that for him, which was probably a good thing.

"My point is that he doesn't always handle his anger and frustration the way others do."

Derrick turned around and watched her pick the soaked edge of her shirt up with two fingers and wave it around a little as if trying to dry it. Another button popped open under the strain of all that flapping. He couldn't imagine that move would dry her shirt, but it sure as hell was making him think about things other than this conversation.

From this angle he could see a sliver of skin and the outline of her bra, all lacy and, from the few peeks she'd given him, pink. This dating, no-touching, possible fake-engagement thing might be the death of him.

"Ellie, I have an office full of Noah types. I don't mind odd comments, social awkwardness or even controllable behavioral issues. But I do get pissed off when people steal from me."

She sat on the couch's armrest. "He insists you're lying."

"And I insist he is."

"So, we're at a stalemate."

"Are we?" He appreciated her loyalty to her brother, but she wore emotional blinders when it came to Noah.

He got it. He had brothers, too. Even though, thanks to their father, they didn't see each other much these days, he would do anything for them, including pushing them to take responsibility for their actions.

"If you had evidence…" With her head down, she picked at the couch's material.

"I'm not accustomed to having to prove myself. Most people take my word." Derrick heard his voice rising in volume and lowered it again. "It's one of those things I'm known for, which is why your brother's actions are doubly problematic."

"Any chance you could bend your rules and maybe…" She winced. "I don't know, review the evidence again? With me?"

It was a fair request but this sudden unexplained need to have her trust hit him. It wasn't rational. He hadn't earned it, but still. "We already have a deal, Ellie."

"I don't appreciate being made to choose."

She wasn't getting this. He pushed off from the counter and walked into the living room area. Stopped right in front of her so she had to look up to give him eye contact. "The point of the agreement is to defuse the issue with the public. Noah will either stop with the videos or he won't."

"And if he doesn't?"

The urge to reach out and brush his fingers over

her cheek almost overwhelmed him. He shoved his hand into his pants pocket to prevent any touching.

It was bad enough he was there. That he had this odd need to see her, to make sure she hadn't changed her mind. He had a phone. He knew how to text. Hell, when he'd first thought about a fake engagement and how it would work, he'd assumed his assistant would be the one in contact with Ellie. That his time with her would be for public view only and a complete farce. Yet, here he was. In her house. Talking family drama.

There was nothing disconnected about this arrangement that he could see.

"With us being together, Noah won't be able to hide from me. I'm confident I can get him to understand. I hired him, young and untested, because I saw something in him." He crossed his arms over his chest and scanned the room, not doing anything to hide his long look. "So...this."

"You're changing the topic." She stood as she talked.

The move put her so close. He could smell the shampoo clinging to her hair and the sharp scent of the wine.

"Obviously." His gaze drifted to her shirt. "Do you want to change?"

"I probably have to throw it away." She winced as she plucked at the material. "And I love this shirt."

He didn't become attached to clothes, so he had no idea how to respond to that. "Go ahead."

Without another word, she slipped into the bathroom, hesitating only long enough to grab a balled-up sweatshirt off the top of one of the boxes piled around the room.

He took the few minutes of alone time to study her apartment again. Tiny and cluttered but homey. There were things everywhere. Shoes piled under the window. A stack of magazines under the coffee table. A... was that a suit jacket on the floor? He scooped it up and draped it over the clean part of the couch. That took him to his next errand. Into the kitchen area to find something to clean up the wine on the cushion.

He was kneeling on the only clean and open part of the floor, doing a combination of dabbing and scrubbing on the stain. He was pretty sure it grew the more he worked on it.

Just as he decided it would be easier to buy her a new couch, she stepped into the room.

"Okay, I'm relatively dry..." Her laser gaze honed in on him right away. "You don't have to do that."

"I know."

"You probably have a team of humans who clean for you."

"Are we fighting again?" He hoped not because there was no way for him to win this battle. She clearly thought he was inept at anything but running a business, and since her brother was trying to ruin that, she might not even find him competent in that regard.

"No, but is there a reason you didn't tell me I had wine in my hair?"

This seemed like slightly safer ground. "I wasn't sure you cared."

She frowned at him. "You are an odd man."

That wasn't a topic he wanted to explore, so he stood with the wet rag still in his hand. "You have two choices."

"You're not planning on testing me on the agreement provisions, are you? I didn't memorize the thing."

Her mind really did bounce from topic to topic. Sometimes it took him a few minutes to catch up. He didn't want to admit that or how invigorating he found the entire verbal battle. "This evening we either can go to dinner or I can help you get packed."

"You make those sound like reasonable options."

She stood right in front of him now. Blame the pink slippers, but he towered over her. She wasn't petite or even short. She likely stood around five-seven. But compared to his six-one, he had the definite height advantage. "I can be reasonable."

"I haven't seen much evidence of that." Her voice took on a breathy quality.

He chalked it up to the room or dust or the boxes or something, because his breathing didn't sound right in his ears, either. "Well, I'm told the early days of fake dating can be rough. We'll both adjust."

"That almost sounded like a joke, but you're not wrong. There really should be a handbook."

"No kidding." He'd be studying that thing nonstop if it did exist.

"Dinner sounds fine, but I know there will be a reporter or photographer lurking somewhere, so what you're proposing is a setup with a side of food."

He sighed at her. "You're paranoid."

"Gee, I wonder why." She added an eye roll as if she didn't think he picked up on the sarcasm dripping from her voice. "And the packing thing…"

Any other time. Any other woman, he wouldn't ask. "Yes?"

The oversize gray college sweatshirt shouldn't even

earn a second of thought from him. But on her, with her sexy mouth and those invigorating comebacks and her refusal to take any crap from him, he got reeled in. She talked and he wanted to know more. He'd studied her background in preparation for making their agreement, but now he wanted to hear the details straight from her, in her time.

"That suggests I'm moving in with you now, and I'm not," she said.

About that…he'd rethought that portion of the agreement. He didn't have much time to meet his father's conditions. His father demanded Derrick get this public fight with Noah wrapped up or he'd lose his chance at owning the company. Never mind that he'd brought it back from the brink of bankruptcy or that the Jameson coffers were now full due to Derrick's efforts. His father insisted, once again, that Derrick prove himself.

There were other conditions about bringing his brothers home and repairing the damage dear old dad had done to his sons' relationships. Derrick liked that part. Running the family business with his brothers and without his father's interference had always been his dream.

But the one issue Derrick had to handle first, the one he'd signed an agreement to fix, related to Ellie. She was the only one he could think about at the moment. That and her mouth and those big eyes.

"We should discuss the timing of your move," he said.

She exhaled long and loud and added another eye roll at the end. "Here we go."

Derrick decided to ignore the dramatics and go

right to the heart of the issue. "You are out of work. Your brother clearly is not contained."

"You aren't exactly wooing me so far."

"I was *telling* you, not trying to convince you."

This time she made a clicking sound with her tongue. "Again with the blind obedience thing. So romantic."

He'd had girlfriends, dated other women, even managed to have sex now and then despite his overwhelming workload. None of that had prepared him for Ellie. He'd never met a woman less impressed with his wealth, position and power than her. It was endearing in some ways but it also messed with his usual way of winning an argument. "Should I call you lovely again?"

"Get to the point."

And now a third eye roll. Great.

He heard a noise and was pretty sure she was tapping her slipper against the floor. In his view, he was the one with the reason to want to move this along, but fine. "We should shift the engagement and—"

"Fake engagement."

"Those are words we only use with each other and when no one else is around."

Her eyes widened as she looked around the room. "Do you see someone else here?"

"I'm just saying." Her glare really could melt stone. He wasn't a fan, but he had to admit it was persuasive. "Fine. Anyway, we should get you settled in."

When he finally got all the words out, she stood there. Silence screamed through the room. Even the foot tapping stopped.

Then… "Wow."

He gave up. "Now what did I say?"

"It's the way you say things. Like, everything is an order."

Damn right. He realized too late he should have made that much more clear in the agreement. "I'm the boss."

"I don't work for you."

"Technically, you do." But he decided not to talk about the fact he was paying for her time, or was about to. She didn't seem to be in the mood to discuss that topic.

"You would be wise not to put this fake engagement in those terms right now."

Yeah, he gave up. "So, dinner?"

She shook her head. "Tomorrow, or maybe the day after. I need a bit of time."

Another zig when he expected a zag. He never thought she'd say no. "Ellie, come on."

"It's not a test." She rested a hand on his chest. "I haven't showered. If people are going to be taking my photograph every two seconds, I should have the opportunity to brush my hair."

He looked down at her fingers and the nails polished a soft pink. Felt the weight of her palm over his heart. "Is this a woman thing?"

"I don't even know what that means."

"Are you still upset about your brother?"

She hesitated then nodded. "Almost always."

"Listen—" Derrick put his hand over hers "—I'll talk to him."

"He'll kill you." And for once she didn't sound excited by the idea.

Still, it wasn't as if he hadn't dealt with trouble before. Compared to the financial crew that wanted to dismantle the company when he became CEO over four years ago and all the fellow businessmen who mistook his youth for weakness, Noah was nothing more than a blip. A small nuisance. "Oh, please."

"I don't think any part of this charade will be as easy as you think it will."

He squeezed her hand. "Trust me."

Six

The DC Insider: *We are concerned, dear readers. It's been five days without a sighting of, or peep about, the most interesting romance in town. Did it already fizzle? There are some nasty whispers out there about the lady's last job. Goodness knows playboy Derrick Jameson has had some interesting things printed about him over the years but it's believed he's put those drinking and carousing days behind him. Maybe Ellie was too wild for her billionaire?*

Derrick sensed Jackson hovering by the door. He'd stepped inside the office but remained quiet. No surprise since Jackson had an uncanny ability to blend in. He overheard more than he should but wasn't the type to start rumors. His loyalty never wavered, which was only one reason Derrick considered Jackson his best friend.

After less than a minute of silence, Jackson cleared his throat. "Is everything okay?"

"With what?" Derrick didn't look up. It was the universal sign for "not now" but he knew Jackson would ignore it.

"Only you would answer that way." Jackson walked into the office. Sat in the chair across from Derrick without waiting for an invitation. "I meant with you... in general."

"I'm fine."

"Is that why you have a woman's shirt in a dry cleaning bag hanging on your office door?"

At the mention of the shirt, Derrick thought about the woman who owned it. Days had passed since they'd talked, and that was no accident. A bit of distance struck him as a smart move. Something about her had him spun around. He wanted her in his home. He'd visited her house for no obvious reason. He never did stuff like that.

"The shirt belongs to Ellie." Not that Derrick wanted to make a big deal about it.

"Yeah, I was hoping you didn't have a second fake fiancée wandering around here."

The comment got Derrick's attention. He settled in his chair as he looked at Jackson. "She had a fight with her brother and spilled wine."

Jackson's eyes narrowed. "Is she okay?"

"In what way?"

Jackson exhaled. "The human way, Derrick."

Derrick had no idea what that meant, but he did get Ellie. At least a little. She played the role of protector. She was the person who came in to clean up the mess, regardless if that meant she didn't have energy left to rescue herself.

"She's overly committed to babysitting her brother. She's been job hunting and I've gotten calls curious about the implications of our relationship. As if I'd get her hired to get the inside scoop on a company. And to top it all off, she's not that excited about moving in with me." The part about her brother should have been the most annoying part, but the last really ticked him off.

"I can't imagine why she doesn't have her bags packed. You're charming."

"It's a big house." Derrick wasn't sure why he needed to keep explaining that.

"Because that was my point." Jackson shook his head as he shifted in his chair. "Is that why you haven't been seeing her? Is she being punished for not jumping to obey your command?"

"What are you talking about?"

"It's as if you're hiding in your office to avoid her... and everything else."

"That's ridiculous." Derrick rubbed his thumb over the leather seam at the edge of the armrest. "I've been slammed with work and am still trying to unravel this Noah mess. It's almost as if he finished his work every day in about an hour and then spent the rest of the time working around our security and protocols and generally searching out every document and email ever sent around here."

"That's scary."

Derrick couldn't disagree with that assessment. "Understatement."

Boredom. That could be the explanation for why Noah had turned on him. Derrick originally assumed greed, but the more he learned about Ellie, inadvertently the more he learned about Noah. From what Derrick could tell, Ellie had eased Noah's way in the world. Maybe too much. It was all something a fake fiancé shouldn't worry about, yet he did. He told himself it was because Noah had stolen from him and he had to fix this, not because he cared.

"He's a genius, right?" Jackson asked.

Derrick was getting tired of hearing that excuse. He knew a lot of really bright people and none of them ever stole from him. "I guess you think that explains his behavior."

"Let's find a new topic. Have you seen the *Insider* today?" Jackson took his cell phone out of his jacket pocket and tapped the screen a few times.

"There shouldn't be anything worth reading about me since I didn't leak a story." Which made him realize he really had ignored Ellie and their arrangement. He should be two steps from putting a fake engagement announcement in the paper. Yet he couldn't pull that trigger, at least not until his brothers hit town and they were on their way.

The hesitancy wasn't based on fear. It was something else…a feeling he couldn't name. This flashing warning signal in his brain that told him to slow down and think things through.

He never expected to want her. This deal was supposed to exist on paper only. He should be able to leave her and not think about her. This whole thing where he wanted to drop by and see her, to call her and talk with her about nothing, made him desperate to create distance between them.

"That's the point. Someone did leak a story and it's not all that flattering to Ellie." Jackson turned his phone around and slid it across the desk toward Derrick.

"What?" Derrick glanced down, skimming the post. Then he read it again. One phrase stuck out: "nasty whispers out there about the lady's last job."

"Damn it."

"You're not the type to let details slip by you, so I'm guessing you knew about Ellie's job issue before you entered into your agreement?"

"Of course. It's all bullshit." He'd made it a point to investigate Ellie before offering her the agreement.

At first, he'd hoped to win her to his side with logic or even bribery, if needed. But the more he'd studied her photo and some bits and pieces of her history, the more the PR firm's offhanded comment about needing an old-fashioned, fake-relationship arrangement to make the Noah problem go away had sounded like the right answer.

And that's how he'd ended up in this mess, wanting her in his bed and at his breakfast table. Smelling her, touching her...tasting her.

"It still sucks for Ellie to have it out there, so public," Jackson said.

"I'll take care of Ellie."

"Did someone mention my name?" Ellie smiled at how the sound of her voice made two grown men freeze in their chairs. Just a handful of words and she had them spinning around and stopping. Now, that was power.

A few seconds later they both continued to stare at her. Jackson recovered first and returned the smile as he rose to his feet. Derrick's reaction was not as welcoming.

"How did you get in here?" Derrick practically barked the question.

Every single day she came up with more things she should have added to their ridiculous agreement. Today? A "no shouting" clause.

"I walked." And she did that again after closing the office door. In a few steps she joined the men by Derrick's desk.

"I'm serious. The protocol and security lapses are starting to annoy me."

Derrick's voice sounded low and growly. She refused to find that sexy. "So, I've been subjected to your nonannoyed personality to date?"

"Ellie." That's it. He said her name in a flat, monotone voice.

He truly was exhausting.

"A very nice woman showed me back. I told her my name and said we were dating—it's weird how much attention that attracted, by the way—and that I needed to talk to you about what was posted in the *Insider*." It had been the first time she talked to anyone about dating Derrick. The way the words had rolled out of her scared her. The lies should have caught in her throat, but no. "I think she took pity on me, probably because I said the part about us dating."

Derrick picked up his phone. "Who was it?"

"Why?"

"She should have called me first."

Truly exhausting. "Then I'm not telling you."

Derrick lowered the handset again. "The person works for me."

Every conversation with him turned into a debate. The few days apart hadn't done anything for his bossiness. She'd hoped he'd also magically turn less attractive. No luck there, either. "The person *helped* me. I'm not tattling on her."

"Tattling?"

She sighed, letting him know she was done with this topic, then glanced over at Jackson. "Did he really forget about dating me like the gossip post said?"

Jackson winced. "That's unclear at the moment."

"Trust me, ignoring you would be impossible," Derrick said.

"It's been days since we signed the agreement, then we had the canceled dinner plans because of your work emergency and then you went into hibernation mode. Even the *Insider* noticed, which is weird because I thought you were the one who fed them their intel."

She'd tried not to let the newest post bother her. Her ex-boss's accusations bordered on horrifying. They were the type to disqualify her for a human resources positions if they were true, which they were not. But no one would care about the veracity of his claims. It was his word versus hers, and now that her supposed relationship with Derrick fueled the town's gossip machine, those untrue accusations would grow even louder.

"Did you need something?" Derrick asked her.

She noticed he skipped right over her comment

about the gossip post. She turned to Jackson for assistance. "Do you think he hears his tone when he talks?"

"I can only hope not." Jackson shook his head. "You should hear him when he actually yells."

She snorted. "No, thanks."

"Ellie!"

This time Jackson laughed. "There, that was close."

Yeah, it looked as if they fully had Derrick's attention now. He held the edge of his desk in a death grip.

Ellie took pity on him. From the exhaustion tugging at the corner of his eyes to the rumpled shirt to the loosened tie, he seemed to be working nearly round the clock after all. "I'm going to ignore the near shouting because I was purposely trying to prick your temper."

"Good Lord. Why?"

She hated to admit it but part of her was testing him. After a few tough years with Noah, running through their parents' life insurance and holding on to the family home only with the help of an aging aunt who lived with them to satisfy a well-meaning social worker, she needed to see if Derrick could control his temper. Then there was the issue of being ignored. "I texted you yesterday and you didn't text back."

Jackson cleared his throat. "So that we're clear, I really want to stay and listen to the rest of this and see how it turns out, but I sense you two need to hash this out without me."

Something in his tone, a mix of amusement and general fondness for Derrick, broke through, making Ellie smile. "Does that mean you'll make him tell you later?"

Jackson nodded. "Definitely."

With a final wink at her and a small nod in Derrick's direction, Jackson took off. He slipped out, closing the door behind him.

"I like him." She did a second glance when something about the door caught her eye. The shirt. The dry cleaning bag.

"I was working."

Derrick's comment dragged her attention to the conversation. She slipped into the seat Jackson had vacated. "Oh, you're answering my previous question now? No texting because you're a busy, busy man?"

"Yes."

"Just so you know, being ignored is frustrating even in a fake dating situation."

For a few seconds Derrick didn't say anything. His gaze searched her face then he leaned into his chair. "I'll do better."

"I'm impressed that's your response." Stunned was more like it. But at his words, she relaxed into the chair, letting her hand fall over the edge of the armrest.

"You strike me as the type who could bolt at any time, so I'm being careful."

Which lead her to another one of the reasons for her visit. "You should know my brother keeps calling me to complain about you. Fair warning, I think another video is coming."

"I'll try to talk to him."

She wanted to believe Derrick could get through to Noah before his behavior spiraled much more. He was fixated on Derrick. Part of her wondered if it was the shock of being fired. But she loved that Derrick promised to try and was holding firm to that vow. Her father used to promise a lot and never follow through. She sensed Derrick was not that kind of man.

"It's not easy to win him over." She hesitated, not sure who much more she should share. "I've tried."

"I get that, but let someone else carry the load for a change."

That sounded so good, so promising, that a wave of relief rolled through her. "We lived together for so long. Right up until he got a job with you and moved into his own studio. Even in college I commuted and went home to him each night."

"You raised him by yourself after you lost your parents?" He sounded horrified at the thought.

"A great-aunt lived with us, which made the court happy. Little did the judge know she chain-smoked, spent her days watching baseball and swearing at the television and was really eighty, even though she looked at least a decade younger." Just thinking about Aunt Lizzy made Ellie smile. "She died my senior year of college. By then I was old enough that the social worker didn't make a fuss."

"You haven't had it easy."

She didn't know anyone who did.

"We have this other thing we need to deal with." She bit her bottom lip as she tried to come up with the right words to describe what really happened. "Joe Cantor. The *Insider* brought up my work history. That can only mean people are whispering about it and making up details... Joe was my boss... He's been saying... I mean, it's not as if it actually happened."

Derrick reached his arm across his expansive desk. "Ellie? Breathe."

She did. "I did not come on to him."

Saying the words brought the frustration crashing down on her again. She had enough to deal with without Joe and his lies. But what she really wanted was to reach out, to grab on to the lifeline Derrick offered. Fighting that urge, she stayed still in the chair.

"Of course not."

"Yeah, that's…" Her brain caught up with the conversation and the air whooshed right out of her body. "Wait, you believe me?"

Derrick's chair squeaked when he got up. Footsteps thudded against the floor as he came around the desk to sit on the edge right in front of her. "Your former boss is a raving jackass."

"I could insert a general snide comment here about businessmen in DC." One that fit a lot of the men she'd met and worked both with and for in the two jobs she'd had since college, the first at a department store then the last one with Joe. But it didn't fit Derrick.

He folded his arms in front of him. "Please refrain."

"I'm stunned you're taking my side. I thought you rich sit-behind-a-desk dudes stuck together."

"And I'm ignoring that description." He continued to watch her. "But the firing was not news to me."

She wrapped her fingers around the edges of the armrests. The wood dug into her palms but she held on. "Technically, I was laid off."

"*Actually*, you were marched out of the office building by security."

She felt something inside her deflate. "Gossip really does run wild in this town."

"There's also rumor you kicked Joe during this argument?" There was no judgment in Derrick's tone. If anything, he sounded amused by the thought.

"Right between the legs." She sighed. "Yeah, that happened."

"Well, there you go."

"Excuse me?"

"Joe is said to enjoy the chase but he clearly doesn't like a woman escalating it to the point of kicking his…"

She laughed. "You can say it."

He smiled at her. Big and beautiful and warm. "Balls."

The amusement died down, leaving behind one unanswered question. "You know about how Joe acts but…"

"What?"

"Are you friends?"

"Hell, no." Derrick made a face that suggested he was appalled at the idea. "And since I hired four women in management positions away from his office years ago, before you were there, he's not my biggest fan."

"You did? I might need their names for my employment attorney. And maybe your testimony."

He nodded. "No problem."

Score one more for Derrick Jameson. He wasn't anything like she expected…well, in some ways, yes. The bossy, intimidating, totally hot part—yes. The kind of sweet side that peeked through now and then? Nope. She had not been prepared for that at all.

"You almost sound likable." More than almost, but that was enough to admit for now.

"Don't start that rumor." He gave her a conspiratorial wink. "Really, though, I'm surprised you lasted with him for more than a day. I can't imagine you taking his nonsense for five seconds without lecturing him to death."

"See, I think there was a compliment in there somewhere, so I'll just say thank you."

"You're welcome." He dropped his arms and let his hands rest on his lap. "And I'm sorry I ignored your text."

"I believe you." But that left one big question. "So, who planted the gossip in the *Insider*? It sounds like someone wants to discredit me."

"I don't know but I'll find out."

An edge had moved into his tone. Usually that sort of thing touched off her guard and her defenses rose. But not this time. She knew the temper wasn't directed at her. "Now you sound angry. Why?"

"Why?"

He sure did enjoy raising his voice. "It's a simple question."

"I don't want anyone messing with you."

"But this is…us…it's fake." She sputtered through the explanation.

"That doesn't mean I want people to spread false rumors about you. How much of a jackass do you think I am?"

"That's kind of sweet."

He frowned at her. "What is?"

"The protective thing. Well, so long as you don't go nuclear about it." She felt obliged to add that caveat since he tended to do things in a *big* way. The last thing she needed was him following her around threatening people.

"Let's say I know what it's like to be on the wrong end of gossip."

Her shoulders fell as some of the comfort that had seeped into her bones seeped right out again. "You're talking about Noah."

"I wasn't." Derrick stood, looming over her. "I don't want to fight with you tonight, and talking about your brother is a guaranteed way to get you fired up."

"What do you want?"

He inhaled deep enough to move his chest up and down. "This."

Then he reached for her. Those strong hands wrapped around her arms and pulled her out of the chair. The move was smooth and gentle; she was on her feet before she even knew what was happening.

He stopped right before kissing her, so she took over. Slipped her arms around his neck and pulled him in closer. He clearly took that as a yes because he regained control from there.

His mouth slid over hers in an explosive kiss that had her pushing up on her tiptoes. Heat washed over her and her muscles went lax. The soft sounds of their kisses mixed with a low grumble at the back of his throat.

This wasn't a test. This kiss lingered and heated. It seared through her, burned a trail right through the heart of her. Stole her breath and left her dizzy and more than a little achy.

When they finally broke apart, her brain had scrambled as her insides turned mushy. Seconds later, she still clung to him, half hanging off him. Those dark eyes searched her face, focused on her mouth, until she could barely breathe.

"Was that to make the engagement seem more real?" The question came out as a whisper. She regretted it a second later, sure that he would use it as an excuse to switch to the cool, in-control Derrick she'd met that first night.

He smiled at her. "Do you think there are cameras in here?"

"I meant were you trying to get me accustomed to kissing you."

"I kissed you because I wanted to kiss you." He skimmed his thumb over her lower lip. "For the record, fake engagement or not, I don't want you to kiss me unless you want to."

"We seem to be stepping into dangerous territory."

"Agreed." He pressed one last quick kiss on her mouth then stepped back. "Dinner?"

The sudden space between them had her emotionally flailing. She tried to act detached. Unaffected. "Okay, is *that* for the fake engagement?"

"You're going to make my head explode."

"Very sexy."

He cupped her cheek and his fingers slipped into her hair. "Yes, you are."

The simple touch, so light, felt so good…and so scary.

This was fake. This was about saving Noah and restoring Derrick's reputation. But still. "Derrick."

"Just dinner. For anything else I'll need a clear green light." He dropped his hand again.

"Wait, do you—"

"Since talking tends to get us in trouble, let's eat." He slipped around to his side of his desk and opened the top drawer. Out came his wallet and keys.

"This feels unsettled." Probably because she wanted

to jump on top of him, wrap her legs around his waist and keep kissing him.

"That's my reaction every second since I met you." He headed toward the door, clearly expecting her to follow him.

She still was not a fan of the way he assumed she'd acquiesce like everyone else seemed to do for him. "Is that my shirt?"

"Well, it isn't mine." He took the hanger off the hook on the door and handed it to her. "Here you go."

She decided to ignore the sarcastic part of his response. "I've been looking for it."

"I had it cleaned."

The bag crinkled in her fingers. "For me?"

"I don't plan to wear it."

It sounded like they were back to the clipped sentences and defensive tone. She wondered if he was going to slip into that mode every time they kissed. "Are you being grumpy because I caught you doing a nice thing?"

"Don't get used to it."

She wasn't sure if he meant the grumpiness or the nice gesture. Right then, she didn't care.

Seven

The DC Insider: *What happens when a nice dinner turns into a near fistfight? We're not sure, either, but we think we came close to witnessing such an event. Rumors have been swirling about Ellie Gold's last job and her unceremonious firing, but Derrick Jameson set us straight. She's the innocent party, he insists. We would have asked more questions but he was busy taking his lady home for the evening—his home.*

Ellie Gold had him completely rattled. Just when Derrick thought he'd figured her out, she said something unexpected. He'd cleaned her shirt—a random, simple thing—and she'd cradled it in her hands as if it were an expensive diamond.

And that kiss.

Before that first one in her apartment about a week ago, he'd planned to keep things on a friendly, non-kissing level. But then his lips had met hers and his brain misfired. He hadn't been able to speak or to think. All he'd wanted to do was to hold on and keep going. He told himself it was because Noah had stolen from him and he had to fix this, not because he cared, but even he was having trouble buying that.

He didn't do overwhelmed. He didn't believe in rainbows or stars or whatever people claimed to see when they experienced a great kiss. He certainly didn't get all breathless and confused when a woman's lips touched his. Not usually, anyway. But with Ellie his body and brain went into free fall.

And it wasn't a onetime thing. The second kiss today nearly scrambled every bit of common sense he possessed. He had been two seconds away from pinning her to the wall and tunneling his hand up that slim skirt when he forced his body to pull back.

She messed him up. Took his balance and his control and ground them into nothing.

Now he watched her study the dinner menu. She even managed to make that look sexy. Her fingers slid along the edge. She lifted her chin as she scanned the page.

He was beginning to think he was losing it.

They sat at a small table near the window of a wildly popular French bistro near Logan Circle. It hadn't been hard to get a last-minute reservation because Derrick had a financial interest in the place. A chance he took on a chef he knew with some of the money he'd stockpiled over the years and it worked out. It also meant there was always room for him. He had to assume the position of the table, out in the open, was the overeager manager's way of capitalizing on his presence there tonight.

People noticed. Quite a few businessmen turned around when he entered the restaurant with Ellie on his arm. Some came over and said hello. One let his gaze linger a bit too long on Ellie's chest for Derrick's liking.

Bottom line—he didn't like being on display. "I feel exposed."

Ellie hummed as she continued to scan the food options. "You picked the game."

"What does that mean?"

"I'm assuming you chose this place, one of the hardest restaurants to get a reservation at right now, to be seen." She peeked at him over the top of the menu. "I'm not even going to ask how you got us in on such short notice. I'll assume this is a case of you being ready at all times for a photo op."

He reached over and lowered her menu so he could meet her eyes without anything getting in the way. "This is dinner, not a photo op."

"That's a first."

"And I'm part owner of this place. The behind-the-scenes money guy."

Her mouth opened a few times before she actually spat out any words. "Well, of course you are."

"Sarcasm?"

"More like *is there any part of this town you don't own* awe." She folded her menu and set it on the space in front of her. "You seem to have an interest in everything."

She was joking but he decided to give her a real

answer. "For the record, I am a minority owner in the family business. My father has the largest stake, and likes to hold that over me. I've tried to branch out with some other investments so I'm prepared."

She frowned. "For what?"

"His whims."

And that's exactly how Derrick saw it. His father played games. He liked to make his sons prove themselves over and over.

Derrick refused to be pushed aside or run off because he viewed the family business as his legacy. He'd worked there during college summers and all throughout business school. After that, he'd come on board full-time and worked his way up. Spent months in every department.

His father demanded perfection and when he didn't get it he'd resort to public humiliation. So, Derrick learned quickly not to make any mistakes. Four years ago his father offered more responsibility and Derrick grabbed at the chance. He'd expanded the family's commercial real estate and construction business and personal holdings.

Ellie watched him for a second then rested her hand on the table. "He's difficult."

"Understatement." Derrick noticed she didn't ask it as a question, so she must have heard at least some of the rumors about his notoriously demanding father. "He put me in charge of expansion, sure I'd fail. He questioned every decision, every strategy. Made it nearly impossible to move forward then yelled because we weren't moving forward."

He was going to say more but stopped. He never talked about family stuff with anyone except Jackson and his brothers. Battling for the business he dreamed of running since he was eighteen was a constant frustration for him. He thought he'd earned it, but no.

"But you eventually convinced him." She leaned in. "You're the big boss now. Right?"

"I'm in charge of the day-to-day operations, but there's no guarantee it's permanent. There are some... things I need to accomplish first." Derrick pivoted off that subject before he divulged something he didn't mean to divulge. "The only reason my father isn't here, picking every move apart, is because he's in love."

Derrick heard the snide edge to his voice but didn't bother trying to hide it. The idea of his father spending his days laughing and drinking after having spent so many years making his sons' lives a constant competition, pitting them against each other and punishing them for any perceived failure, rubbed Derrick raw.

Ellie blinked. "Excuse me?"

"Wife number four."

"Oh." Ellie's mouth dropped open. "Do we like her?"

"Thanks to Jackie, my father is testing out possible retirement far away on a beach in Tortola." He laughed. "So, yes."

"Your family is not dull."

No kidding. "And since you commented on my businesses, you should know I have no financial interest in the gas station across the street. I wish I did because I think my tank is almost empty."

"You'll probably buy that next week."

Since she sounded amused by his comments he played along, happy to move off a subject that kept him up at night worrying. Off the fear his father would show up and take it all away without warning. Derrick would survive, of course, but he wanted the family business and the family that went with it. "If I find some extra time at lunch to buy a multimillion-dollar venture, sure."

"Ellie."

Her smile disappeared as she looked up at their unwanted dinner guest. "Mr. Cantor."

Joe Cantor, Ellie's former boss, stood at the edge of the table. A guy known to have a wandering eye and a big mouth. He wasn't half the businessman he thought he was. The only thing that saved him was a mix of old family money and a forgiving wife. As far as Derrick was concerned, the wife could do a lot better than Joe—a man still trying to live off his former reputation as a big-man-on-campus almost two decades later.

Joe glanced at Derrick then focused on Ellie again. "I've been reading about the two of you."

Yeah, Derrick was done. "And I've been reading about you."

Joe's eyes narrowed. "What?"

"I thought you'd like to explain why Ellie was fired." Derrick didn't bother lowering his voice. He wanted people to know how little he thought about Joe's fake dismissal story. "Right here. To my face. In front of her. Let her finally tell her side."

Joe's smirk didn't waver. "Look, it's over. You two are together now."

"Clearly." Before tonight Derrick didn't think much of Joe. Now he thought even less. This intimidation tactic was a clear misstep. A smart guy wouldn't have tried it.

"Whatever happened between us—"

"Nothing." Ellie's eyebrow lifted as she stared Joe down. "Nothing happened between us. Ever."

Joe shook his head. "Ellie, it's okay. It's done."

"Not really." Derrick hated this guy now. "She's still waiting on your apology."

For the first time Joe's mouth fell into a flat line. "What?"

"I don't like when people make up stories about my woman."

Ellie made a humming noise. "*My woman*? Do we like that phrase?"

"Too much?" Derrick asked, seeing in Ellie's eyes that she was enjoying Joe's public takedown. Derrick looked at Joe again, who didn't appear as smug now. "Then ignore the word choice, but the result is the same. One more false word about her coming on to you—which we both know is complete bullshit—and you get to fight me."

Joe let out a pathetic strangled laugh and did a quick glance around. "Are you threatening me, Derrick?"

"I'm actually threatening your business. I thought that was obvious." He glanced at Ellie. "No?"

She put her hand over his. "I thought you were very clear."

"Thank you, dear." Derrick winked at Ellie then turned to Joe again. "Clean up the *misunderstanding* about her firing and then keep your mouth shut, and we're good. Maybe she'll even decide not to sue you."

She shrugged. "I can't promise that."

Joe glared at Derrick. "You can't be serious."

"We're done here." Derrick slid his hand out from under Ellie's and picked up his menu again. "You hungry? I am."

Joe closed in on Ellie. "Tell him the truth."

She didn't even flinch. "Your wife went out of town, you came on to me, I kicked you and then I got fired."

"That's not—"

"Illegal?" More than one table of restaurant patrons was watching now. The manager even made a move toward the table, but Derrick gave a small shake of his head to keep him back. He had this handled. "Yes, Joe. I think it is."

She shrugged. "My lawyer says it is."

Fury flashed in Joe's eyes. "You can't outlast me and you know it."

Ellie deserved better and this show. Even though they kept it respectable, Derrick knew the gossip would make the rounds. They'd proved their point. Now it was time for Joe to get the message and slink away. "For us, it's a date. For you? This is a chance to move without increasing your liability. I'd take it."

Joe gave them one last stare then turned and walked off. He was smart enough to not cause a bigger scene or to storm away. He slipped through the tables with a smile on his face as if they'd been having a nice dinner talk.

The second after he was gone the restaurant's noise level rose again. People seated nearby returned to eating and servers ran around getting food and drinks to the crowded tables.

When Derrick finally glanced across the table

again he saw Ellie staring at him. A smile played on her lips. A sexy smile that jolted through him.

"That was thoroughly satisfying," she said.

"Now that's the sort of thing I like to hear from a date."

The rest of the dinner consisted of talking and some verbal sparring, but the fun kind. Ellie finished her meal in a satisfied haze. She enjoyed letting her guard down and ignoring all the stress for an hour.

After her parents died she'd juggled college and Noah. She'd waded through their mess of an estate. All those failed ventures her father had started and driven into bankruptcy. All the debts that had to be paid and the questions people had looked to her to answer.

She'd handled all of it. Put her personal life on hold, limited dating to brief flings and friendships to a minimum. She'd worked hard, kept her head down and never expected anything from anyone. That's why her friendship with Vanessa meant so much.

Vanessa was the kind of best friend you could call in the middle of the night and she'd come running. She was smart and supportive. They could sit in silence for hours and watch movies. Gossip. Ellie was comfortable around Vanessa when Ellie wasn't all that comfortable with most people. Not on a deep level. Not enough to trust.

It's why Derrick's near automatic defense took Ellie by surprise. For the first time in ages, she had someone other than Vanessa looking out for *her*. Willing to stand up to someone else and protect her from the fallout. Willing to take care of her. It was a heady and humbling feeling.

That was the only explanation she had for why she stood in the middle of his kitchen at after nine that night instead of in her apartment. That and the fact she wanted to be there. Wanted to spend time with him. Wanted to know more about the man who fought so hard against his father.

She'd seen the stark ache in Derrick's eyes at dinner as he talked about the business. He tried to joke about finances, but she'd heard the roughness in his voice. She tried to imagine what it was like to be the oldest son of a man who enjoyed demeaning people, including his own children.

They'd walked in from the garage with the lights clicking on as they'd moved through the high-ceilinged, expertly-carved-moldings, man-this-is-expensive Georgetown house. Even in the dark she had seen rows of impeccably kept brick town houses as they'd driven through the tree-lined streets. The whole area dripped with wealth.

By the time they'd pulled off a narrow street and into Derrick's garage—a thing she didn't really think existed in this part of town outside of huge mansions—she'd confirmed she was way out of her league.

Now she looked around the pristine kitchen with the gray cabinets and swirling white-and-gray-marble countertops that looked like they should be on the cover of some fancy home magazine. Not a pot out of place. Not a glass in the sink.

For the fourth time since they'd left the restaurant, confusion crashed into her. She'd been riding this emotional roller coaster for most of her life but with

Derrick the ride turned wild. She flipped between interest and frustration. One minute she wanted to kiss him. The next, punch him.

They were supposed to be in a business arrangement and nothing more. But those kisses and the way he touched her, looked at her…how her heart thundered in her ears when he smiled. How she wanted to peel away the layers and peek beneath to see the real man.

Her attraction to him in more than an objective "oh, he's good-looking" way was unexpected and kind of unwanted. It clouded everything. They were from different worlds and using each other. But the glimpses she'd seen weren't of a thoughtless playboy who liked to throw money around. He was deeper than that. Far too likeable. Very tempting.

She sat on the stool at the massive kitchen island then stood again. "I feel like we're inviting trouble being here alone."

"You're going to be moving in here soon." Derrick took off his suit jacket and loosened his tie. Next he reached for one of the big double doors to the refrigerator and brought out two bottles of water. "You should get used to the place."

"Not that soon."

He set the bottles next to her on the countertop. "I'm thinking within days."

"I'm saying within weeks." She tried to mentally slam the brakes on all of this. The move, the engagement, the agreement. If the attraction she felt for him was real, should she really mix in the parts that weren't? She really didn't know anymore.

Life whizzed by her so quickly since she'd met him.

Her brain rushed to keep up, but when that failed, her emotions took over. Her wants and needs won out. She wanted him to touch her again. To give in and take something for herself for a change.

"You really do thrive on being difficult," he said.

She thought they were well matched on that score, but she didn't bother to argue since that would only prove his point. "Maybe, but I'm still grateful."

He put his hands on the counter on either side of her, trapping her there in a warm cocoon. "For what?"

Tension spun up inside her. She knew she could break out of his hold but the problem was she didn't want to. That's how little it took. He moved in, close enough for her to smell the soap on his skin, and her heartbeat took off in an all-out race. She wanted to run her fingers over the light stubble on his chin. Feel his mouth on hers.

She fought for breath as she pretended to stare at the white farmhouse sink behind him. "Look at this kitchen. My entire apartment would fit in here."

His gaze searched hers until she looked at him again. "For what, Ellie?"

"What you said to Joe. How you stuck up for me without making me prove my side of the story." She gave in to the need to touch him then. Let her fingers trail over his tie, follow it to the end and hang there. "For the nice dinner."

"I don't want your gratitude."

Her stomach took off on a frenzy of somersaults. "What do you want?"

"You."

The deep voice, having that laser-like focus trained on her, the combination pushed the fight out of her.

She'd been running and making excuses and coming up with arguments. But there, staring up at him, seeing the intensity in those eyes, she gave in.

She tugged on his tie and brought him in even closer. The air between them burned with a new energy. His mouth met hers and the rest of the world blinked out.

Heat roared through her as his lips crossed hers. Firm kisses. The sweep of his tongue over hers. One minute she stood there and the next he lifted her onto the counter. Her tight skirt bunched high on her thighs as he pushed them apart to stand between them.

His hands roamed over her back then to her neck. Fingers slid through her hair. His touch managed to be soothing and demanding at the same time. Heat radiated off him as she unknotted his tie. And when his mouth moved to her cheek then to her ear, a shiver stole her balance. She fell hard against him as his tongue traced a line down her neck.

They both made hungry, growling sounds and she ached for more. Her heels closed around his thighs, tightening his body against hers.

"Ellie?"

"Yes. Green light." She caught his mouth again. The kiss seared through her, destroying her worries.

His hands skimmed around her body, over her breasts. She almost sighed in relief when she felt his fingers on her shirt buttons. The voice inside her head screamed for him to hurry, but a part of her wanted to savor every minute. Every lingering touch.

"Oh, damn. Sorry!"

The deep male voice rang out in the kitchen. Ellie heard it but it took her another few seconds to realize what was happening.

Someone was there, in the house. As soon as that thought registered in her brain, she shoved against Derrick's chest. Their legs tangled together and his hand got caught in her shirt. When he stepped to the side, turned around and stood in front of her like a human shield, he almost ripped her silk blouse.

Derrick's shoulders went from stiff to relaxed as he looked at the intruder. "Spence?"

She didn't have the same reaction as she worked in double time to line up her shirt buttons and get them closed again.

The other man held up a hand but he didn't try to hide his smile. "I can leave."

"Of course not." Derrick glanced at her over his shoulder. His gaze bounced to her shirt and he nodded before stepping to the side and helping her from the counter. "Ellie Gold, this is one of my brothers, Spencer."

She grabbed for her skirt and tugged it down before she gave his brother an unexpected show. "Right."

Heat flamed in her cheeks. She could only imagine the force of her blush, but she pushed through and gave him eye contact. She should have done that first because she would have known the two men were related.

Spencer was a slightly stockier version of Derrick. They both towered over her and were blessed with that's-almost-unfair good looks. The Jameson family had a heck of an impressive gene pool. Their father might be a jerk but he churned out dark-haired hotties without trouble.

Spencer's smile reached his eyes, which made her think he did it more than his brother. That might also explain the lightness about him. Derrick walked around as if he carried the responsibility for the world on his shoulders. Spencer didn't give off that vibe.

"I'm Spence." He held out his hand. "The middle Jameson brother."

Derrick snorted as they shook hands. "The one with the shitty timing."

"I didn't know… See, Derrick never really brings… Okay then." Spence made a hissing sound. "I'll stand here and not talk."

His stumbling eased her discomfort at having been caught like a naughty teen on prom night. "What were you trying not to say?"

"He's pointing out that I'm not in the habit of bringing women to my house," Derrick said.

Spence nodded. "Yeah, that."

"Ellie is different." Derrick picked up one of the water bottles off the counter and offered it to her. "She's moving in."

Spence's eyes grew even wider. "Really?"

She waited for Derrick to explain about the agreement and Noah and all the trouble they were trying to fix. When Derrick didn't say anything, she glanced over at him. "And?"

He wrapped an arm around her shoulders. "We're still fighting over the date."

Her mind jumbled again. "Wait…"

"Ah, now I get it," Spence said.

That made one of them. She was still lost. "Want to explain it to me?"

Derrick moved then. He put down the water and reached for his suit jacket. His keys jangled in his hand a second later. "Let me run Ellie home then we'll catch up."

Spence frowned. "She's the one who should stay."

She wanted some air…and an explanation. "No, it's fine." She glanced at Derrick, sending him a we-need-to-talk glare. "You ready?"

If she knew her way around the house she would have taken off without him. Instead she followed him along a hallway and a set of stairs to the bottom level of the grand three-story home.

Her head was pounding too hard for her to concentrate but as soon as they were in the garage with the door shut behind them, she spun around to confront Derrick. "Your brother doesn't know."

He had the nerve to stare at his keys and not her. "About what?"

She put her hand over his. "That this is a fake arrangement, Derrick."

"It didn't feel fake a second ago." He hit her with intense eye contact. The kind that made her breath catch in her throat.

"I refuse to regret that."

"I hope not since I'm planning on finishing it very soon." He blew out a long breath. "Look, if you can't tell your brother, I can't tell mine. That seemed fair to me."

He said it as if the logic made perfect sense. She didn't buy it. Jackson knew. She had every intention of telling Vanessa when they met for lunch tomorrow as planned. She had no idea how she held it in this long, except that Vanessa had gone away on a work trip for four days.

No way did Derrick's brother need to be kept in the dark about something this big. He should know he wasn't really about to get a sister-in-law. "I hate when you sound reasonable because it convinces me you're hiding something."

"I think our agreement makes it clear we both are."

It was hard to argue with that. "Okay, but when it comes to this agreement and what we both get out of it, we'll be honest with each other, right? We need each other, and I'm not talking about the kissing."

"I'm happy to talk about the kissing."

Her stomach did a little tumble. "I'm not kidding, Derrick."

"Trust me."

He made it sound so easy, but he had no idea. Her father used to say that, too. *We'll be fine, Ellie. This time the plan will work. You won't have to switch schools.* Then he broke the promises almost as quickly as he made them.

"You've been in charge and getting your way for too long." She'd thought that from the first minute she'd met him and she still believed that was true.

"I have a feeling that's about to change."

Sounds as if he was finally getting it. "Count on it."

Eight

The DC Insider: *There is a lot happening in the Jameson household these days. Middle brother and perennial black sheep, Spencer, has returned to the nest. Does that mean baby brother Carter is on his way? Bigger question: if the family is coming into town, do Derrick and Ellie have big news to share?*

Derrick couldn't fight off the very strong feeling he'd screwed things up tonight. He didn't regret kissing Ellie, touching her. Hell, he'd been five seconds away from slipping her underwear off and carrying her upstairs when Spence showed up.

Them in bed. Sex. All that was going to happen. When he'd first met her, he'd thought he could keep the attraction separate, but since it sparked both ways, why fight it? They could enjoy each other, help each other with their family issues and have a good time. Win, win.

The only problem, as usual, came from his father. Those damn requirements of his. The ones that stood between Derrick and the business he'd always wanted.

In Derrick's head it made sense to hide from Ellie the fact that he could lose the business. Why give her that much power over him? It also made sense to hide the fake engagement part from Spence and Carter, because they would never agree with his decision to make that choice.

But all the half-truths, the partial information, meant lying to the people around him. He'd never out-and-out deceived his brothers before. Sure, when they were younger, he'd downplayed their father's crappy actions and how poorly he'd treated their mom before she died. What kind of man went to his wife's deathbed and asked for a divorce so he could marry his mistress sooner?

This was different. He wasn't protecting them as much as trying to handle everything his own way without interference. He worried that made him the asshole this time.

"So." Spence made the word last for three syllables. "I think you left something out of our weekly phone call. We talked about Dad's stupid business agreement, but I don't remember you mentioning Ellie."

That call was a tradition Derrick would not let die. Their father had tried to drive the brothers apart by making them compete over everything from sports to his affection. Derrick refused to let the bond break. He hadn't always been a great brother. At times he'd outright failed at keeping the family running, but Carter and Spence mattered to him and losing them was not an option. Ever.

They were both welcome in his house anytime. He'd bought a five bedroom so they'd have a place to stay when they were in town. Carter rarely came in from the West Coast. Not since the huge falling-out with their father over the running of the family estate in Virginia—the Jameson property no Jameson currently lived in.

Spence had been bouncing around from place to place, but stopped in for a few days now and then. His timing kind of sucked this time because Ellie was moving in and the fake engagement was moving forward. Having Spence there and not telling him the whole story would only make that all the more awkward.

"Ellie was a surprise." Derrick turned the words over in his head and decided that might be the most truthful statement he'd ever made.

"Women are like that."

Derrick leaned against the sink, facing Spence. "Not for me. Not usually."

"So, let me get this straight." Spence balanced his palms on the counter behind him. "Right now you're dealing with Dad and the business. He's insisting you bring Carter and me home or he'll sell it out from under you."

That was the biggest of the moving parts. "About that—"

"Wait, I'm not done." Spence paused, as if he needed more drama here. "Some kid has launched a campaign to paint you as a...what, bad boss? And on top of that and all the work you're putting in you found time to date. And not just date, to seriously date for the first time in…ever, right?"

That about summed it up. "Yes."

"Anything else I should know? Like maybe you invented something or cured cancer while I was gone."

"Ellie is his sister." That much Derrick could tell. Maybe Spence would have some ideas on how to shut down Noah without ticking off Ellie, because Derrick hadn't come up with one yet.

"Now you've lost me."

"The guy who worked for me, the one who stole, but insists I fired him out of spite and that I'm completely incompetent. His name is Noah and he's Ellie's little brother."

Spence whistled. "You do like to make your life as shitty as possible, don't you?"

"He's how I met Ellie."

"And now you're going to be living together."

"Yes." Unless she killed him first, which Derrick thought was a strong possibility.

"You, who has only ever introduced me to the women you dated after you stopped dating them and once they've moved into friend mode."

"I'm a complex guy."

Spence shook his head. "I'm not sure that's the word I'd use."

"Ellie is…" Man, Derrick didn't even know what to say next. Hot, special. Annoying yet energizing. He didn't get her at all or understand her hold on him. All he knew was that she'd flipped his life upside down and had him scrambling, and that a part of him enjoyed the chaos. "Different."

Derrick thought he found a nice, safe description until Spence frowned at him. And stared...then kept staring. "What?"

Spence made a groaning sound. "You should work on that."

"What?"

"How you describe Ellie and your feelings for her. An orange car is different. Your girlfriend should warrant a better word." Spence glanced at the very spot where Ellie had been on that counter. "If you plan to make out with her in the kitchen again, that is."

Oh, that was definitely happening. Derrick didn't even have to think about that. Forget hands-off and common sense. The next time he'd lock the door and strip her clothes off. "I was doing fine."

"I think I arrived just in time."

That's not how Derrick saw the situation at all. "Two hours from now would have been better."

Spence stepped away from the counter and headed for the living area off the kitchen. "Well, since neither of us is having sex tonight, you may as well fill me in."

"On what?"

"Ellie. I want details." Spence sank into one of the couches set up in front of the massive stone fireplace. "I can get them from you or I can ask her."

"Subtle."

"Start talking."

Breakfast with Vanessa went great, as usual, until Ellie mentioned Derrick and dating and the whole *big lie for good press* thing. Amazing how that brought all of the other conversations to a standstill. Even now, twenty minutes later as they walked to Ellie's apartment, Vanessa barely said anything.

Ellie was about to make a joke about how her timing of the news messed up any chance at getting more coffee when Vanessa finally piped up. "A fake engagement."

They turned the corner at the end of Ellie's block and headed toward her building. "I know it sounds ridiculous."

"You mean like we've stepped into some weird novel? Yeah."

"It's the best option for Noah."

Vanessa stopped stared at Ellie. The look on her face hinted at the confusion pinging around inside her.

"What about what's best for Ellie?" Vanessa asked.

That wasn't the reaction Ellie expected. Yelling, yes. Even a few well-placed "Are you out of your mind?" comments. But that? No. "What does that mean?"

"We need to talk about your propensity to look out for everyone but yourself." Vanessa sounded furious at the idea.

Cars whizzed by and Ellie could see the stoplight in the distance. She wanted to focus on all of that and drown out the voice inside her head that told her she was getting in deep with Derrick. That she would never be able to keep sex and her attraction separate from her growing feelings for him. That, most troubling of all, she was starting to like him and was desperate to spend time with him.

She focused on the practical instead. "I need a job, security and some relief from the ongoing Noah drama. Derrick provides that."

"At the risk of violating the Bechdel test and talking only about men, isn't Derrick the reason Noah is spinning right now?"

"I used to think so."

"And now?"

"As Derrick keeps reminding me, Noah is an adult. He's had therapy and needs to figure out how to control the frustration when it tries to overtake him. He won't be able to survive in the work world otherwise." Ellie hated to admit that.

After all these years of guiding him and handling the oppositional defiant disorder so that it didn't morph into something even more serious, she had to start to back away. Not completely. She'd always be there for him, but he needed to be in charge of his behavior and take responsibility for his actions. It was time to let him make mistakes like everyone else.

Even now he texted and called every day. He insisted he was about to break some new story about Derrick. Something awful that would make her see the man he really was. She begged him not to and so far he hadn't, but she sensed it was only a matter of time.

Vanessa exhaled and some of the concern seemed to leave her face. "Well, if Derrick convinced you to give Noah some space, then I might learn to like him, though I'm not promising."

Of course Vanessa liked the comment because she'd been suggesting the same thing for a while now.

"Derrick also went after Joe Cantor."

Vanessa smiled and started walking again. "I know. I read the *Insider*."

Ellie almost choked. "Good grief, why?"

"It's wildly entertaining. If I had known the business world was so full of gossip and sex, I might have traded in some of my art history classes for economics."

They dodged a group of men loading boxes into a truck and jogged up the steps to the front of her building. Kept going past the mailboxes and the elevator that seemed to be stuck with an open door and not moving.

"Derrick keeps planting stories. And now someone else is." She could barely handle Derrick's PR campaign, though she had to admit he had eased off a bit. Photographers weren't lurking around capturing pictures of them every second, as she once feared. But the *Insider* still churned out tidbits about their dinners and her movement every time she stepped outside.

"Who else?"

"Joe, more than likely." And that was the bigger concern. Someone wanted to discredit her. Derrick had vowed to stop it. But what happened to her once he was done with their fake arrangement? She still had to work. To eat. To find a real job.

Her stomach tumbled and a wave of nausea battered her. She wanted to think it related to the very real fear of not being able to support herself in the future, but she sensed it had something to do with the idea of waking up one day and not seeing Derrick again. Of losing the talking and arguing and zap of attraction that struck her whenever she saw him.

"The men in your life are exhausting," Vanessa said.

They turned the corner and moved into the hallway leading to her apartment door. Ellie reached for her keys and nearly dropped them. "Tell me about it."

Vanessa stopped in midstep. "What's going on?"

Ellie's head shot up. Her front door was open and two boxes were piled right outside in the hall. Panic surged through her as she ran to the doorway. "Hey!"

She didn't go in. There really was no reason to since the room, her studio, stood empty except for a few stray pieces of paper and what looked like a community of dust bunnies she'd missed living under her couch.

"Did you get evicted?" Vanessa asked, her gaze zooming from one end of the room to the other.

"No." At least she didn't think so.

Her mind flashed to the van outside. To the packed boxes. To the movers.

Derrick.

"Good afternoon." Jackson stepped out of her bathroom, carrying her robe.

Ellie wasn't sure what stunned her more, him being in her apartment or the sight of him holding a ball of pink fluff in his arms. "Jackson?"

"You know him?" Vanessa asked.

"He works for Derrick. They're friends..." Ellie didn't know how to describe their relationship. She knew Jackson was loyal to Derrick but there was a part of her that viewed him as an ally. Or she had until this. "It's complicated."

"Most things with Derrick are." Jackson put down the robe and shook Vanessa's hand.

Vanessa stared at their joined hands then at Jackson. Finally she shrugged. "What's happening?"

Jackson frowned. "Ellie is moving in to Derrick's place today."

He said the words slowly, as if he thought they were true at one time but now wasn't sure. Ellie blamed

Derrick. He had that effect on her, as well. "I didn't agree to do that now."

"He said…" Jackson's frown deepened. "Wait, you guys didn't agree today was the day? Then where did he get the key he gave me?"

"Good question." If Ellie had to guess she'd bet he somehow convinced her landlord to turn one over. Or he bought the building and now *was* her landlord.

"I figured you weren't here and weren't packed up because Derrick told you I'd handle it."

Yep, this was definitely Derrick's fault. He ordered and manipulated. Looked like Jackson got stuck in his trap this time, too.

"I'm going to kill him." Ellie had threatened it before but this time she just might do it.

Jackson swore under his breath. "I'll take that as a no. Derrick did this all on his own."

Ellie shouldered part of the blame. A very small part. She'd let Derrick lure her in. He did nice things for her. He kissed like he'd been born to do it. All that stopped now. She needed some control and she would wrestle him for it, if needed. "I'll handle this."

"Are you sure?" Jackson looked as skeptical about her statement as he sounded.

"Yeah, really?" Vanessa gestured toward Jackson. "Listen to him."

She got it. Vanessa was fighting a bout of friendly concern. Jackson likely thought this was one step too far, even for Derrick. They were both right and she appreciated it, but she and Derrick had an agreement. She also thought they had an understanding and possibly something bigger that might lead to getting naked.

"If Derrick wants a showdown, we'll have one."

This time Vanessa looked skeptical. Also a bit worried. "Is this a good idea? Derrick isn't exactly a lightweight. I'm guessing he barges in and gets his way a lot."

Ellie couldn't deny that, but he wouldn't hurt her. His yell didn't even scare her that much. No, this was about Derrick Jameson understanding how far he could push her. And he'd gone too far. "He needs to learn."

Jackson hadn't moved. It was as if he were rooted to that spot on her floor. "True, but…"

"I'm looking forward to meeting Derrick," Vanessa said. "Sounds like the guy needs a good kick."

Vanessa wasn't wrong on that, either. Ellie vowed to be the one who administered the blow.

"You will soon enough." Ellie looked at Jackson. "I need your help."

"I almost hate to ask what for." But he smiled.

"You'll see."

Nine

The DC Insider: *Living together? Why, Derrick Jameson. You are a fast worker. And, Ellie? You're our hero. Tame that rowdy billionaire.*

Jackson didn't sound an alarm unless something was really wrong. So, when he called from Derrick's house, insisting there was a problem, Derrick got his butt over there and fast.

Driving up outside, everything looked normal. The usual cars on the street. Nothing odd in his driveway. It wasn't until he got out of the garage and reached the bottom of the stairs to the main living area that he heard the deafening thumping. He didn't know how he'd missed it earlier.

Music. Blaring music.

After marching upstairs, he turned the corner and

stepped into the open kitchen and living room area…
and stopped. Both the television and stereo were on,
and at what sounded like full power. Magazines were
strewed all over his usually clutter-free space. There
were open boxes and balled-up piles of clothes. Books
everywhere. He couldn't see an inch of his hardwood
floor.

Ellie sat in the middle of it all, sprawled on his
couch with her feet propped up on the coffee table.
She wore a pink robe and matching slippers. Ate po-
tato chips right out of the bag. Drank…was that red
wine? One wrong move and his light gray couch, the
one he'd owned for less than a year, wouldn't survive
the alcohol bath.

It took a few seconds for her to stop her off-key
singing and look up at him. "Hey, roomie."

So that's what this was. Payback. He had to give
her credit because little surprised him and this did.
He'd expected a series of nasty texts or an office visit.
Not this.

To avoid yelling over the song he didn't recognize,
he went to the stereo and turned it off. That left the
talk show, which raged in a circus of screaming. He
scanned the stacks of crap for his remote and didn't
see it. Realizing he had no idea how to turn the television off without it, he gave in. "Any chance you could
take care of that?"

She pretended not to hear. Put her hand behind her
ear, leaned in and everything. Apparently full drama
mode had been activated.

He tried again. "Turn. It. Off."

"Oh, sure." She reached under the chip bag and
produced the remote. The noise clicked off a second

later. "I'm recording this, anyway. Actually, I'm recording a lot of programs." She studied the remote and its buttons. "Did you know your DVR is empty? There's plenty of room for my stuff."

He inhaled, trying to hold on to the fleeting sense of control he'd had when he'd started the day. "I don't watch much TV."

"Then it's good I rented a whole bunch of movies. Your on-demand options are impressive."

He could hardly wait to see that bill. "Are you done?"

"Enjoying the house? Not even close." She continued to sit there with one leg crossed over the other, her pink slipper bouncing up and down.

The robe slipped, treating him to miles of toned thigh. When she didn't rush to close the material again, a new sensation hit him. She was making a point but she might also be making a play.

Now he needed to know what she had on under there and how long it would take him to peel it off her.

But he forced his mind to focus. He looked around again, wondering how long it had taken her to make this much mess and how many days it would take him to undo it. "I'm assuming this is your way of saying you don't appreciate the manner in which I moved you in here."

Even he had to admit he'd crossed a line, but he wasn't up for a debate about something he thought should be simple. Today, Spence had agreed to come into the office for a few hours, and Derrick knew Ellie had made plans to spend a few hours with Vanessa. It struck him as the perfect time to get the job done.

He'd taken care of it all, which meant delegating to

Jackson. The bigger benefit—he thought—was shutting down Ellie's attempts to stall by complaining about packing.

The plan may have worked if he hadn't gotten tied up in a meeting that ran long. He'd planned to meet up with Ellie *before* she'd headed to her apartment. To warn her. That had failed.

"Derrick, this is better than any hotel." She wore one of those sickeningly sweet smiles that silently telegraphed her desire to push someone in front of a speeding bus. "I plan to stay right here. And I mean *right here*. In this spot. With my boxes stacked all around me as I collect more and more stuff. Now that I know the official address for your house I can have even more boxes delivered."

"Okay, I get it."

Her head fell to the side as she stared up at him. "Do you?"

He should be furious or at least frustrated. He was turned on. Like, ten-seconds-from-stripping-that-robe-off-her turned on.

What he should do is explain the reason for his actions then get back to work. End any temptation and not go near her.

All good thoughts…smart. But he didn't intend to do any of it. No, they were going to be naked and soon. Her legs wrapped around him. Her mouth on his. The wall, the couch, the floor. He didn't care where so long as they got there soon.

He walked over to her. Maneuvered through the piles and kicked aside more than one stray shoe. No question her entire closet now rested on his floor.

She didn't bother to move the chips or the pillows

she had stacked on one side of her, so he picked the coffee table. Sliding some books aside, he sat across from her, right next to her legs.

Through it all, she watched him. Her expression bordered on a smile. A satisfied one. Clearly she enjoyed this moment and the statement she was making.

That seemed fair, because he was a reluctant fan, too. "I may have been a little heavy-handed in my approach to making your relocation happen."

She rolled her eyes. "Saying 'I'm sorry' would have been a shorter sentence."

He held in a smile. "True."

"Do you want to try it? I promise it won't hurt at all." Her voice dipped lower, grew sexier, as she finally put aside the chips and the magazine and folded her hands on her lap.

His mind went back to that robe. Her long, sexy legs were right next to him. He glanced over, taking in the bare skin and those muscles, all sleek and sexy. Suddenly he had only one question...

"What are you wearing under that?"

Amusement danced in her eyes as she reached for the belt and untied it. The slow reveal had his heart hammering in his chest. She must have sensed it because she took her time peeling the sides apart to reveal a pair of running shorts and a formfitting tank top. On her, the combination was just about the hottest thing ever.

His gaze traveled down her neck and over the slope of her shoulder. To her chest. Had she skipped the bra?
Damn...

She snapped her fingers. "That apology?"

Maybe it was the way she sat there, looking ready

to do battle, but his usual hate-to-lose-at-anything armor fell. "I should have talked to you first."

Silence thumped between them after he ended the sentence. For a few seconds they sat there.

"That's it?" she asked.

"Yes."

She sighed at him. "Try again."

Apparently his defenses hadn't fallen far enough for her liking. "I was attempting to honor our agreement."

"For the record, you're getting farther away from an actual apology, not closer." She glared at him.

He was surprised she didn't have a headache from doing that. "You said—"

"Nope."

On anyone else the refusal to back down would piss him off. He liked to be in control, to come out on top of any argument. But he loved that she pushed him. She didn't try to impress him. She didn't need to try because she did it naturally, just by sitting there.

He conceded this point to her, expecting it to cost him something. For it to grate against his nerves. "I apologize for unilaterally making the decision. I should have conferred with you."

Once it was out there, he waited for a kick of frustration to nail him. He should be running to work. He didn't spend afternoons hanging around at home. Hell, he spent most nights at his desk. Until he'd met her, that was the only answer. Push forward, drive in more business. But now, today, he was perfectly content to sit and look at her, to wait to see what she would say next.

Lately his frustration with his father's demands, the needs of the company, his brothers and his own instincts were pulling him in too many directions. Ellie cleared away all the noise and stress and let him relax. It had been a long time since he'd felt comfortable in his own skin—then again, it wasn't really comfort he was feeling.

But he was holding back details. They'd agreed to be honest with each other, but he hadn't told her all of it. She didn't know that him being successful in calming Noah down was part of a bigger plan to win the business. That, in reality, he needed her. He hated needing anything but this time he did.

"That sounded more like a presentation to your bankers than a real apology, but I'll take it."

He finally let out that laugh he'd been holding inside. Leave it to her to judge his apology and sincerity and find both lacking.

He glanced around. "So, how exactly did you make all this happen in such a short amount of time?"

"I told your movers to leave the boxes here then I dumped the contents all over your living room."

Joe Cantor was an idiot to fire her. If he'd harnessed her drive and talent, his business would be doing much better today. Derrick would bet the Jameson water properties on it. "By yourself?"

"It was my idea but I asked Jackson to help."

The idea of Jackson and Ellie teaming up against him hit Derrick like a shot to the chest. He would stand almost no chance against their joint forces. But he did like that they seemed friendly, that Jackson was protective of her.

Still, he was the boss and there should be limits, at least in theory. "He's fired."

"We both know that's not true."

He peeked at her legs again. Followed the long line to her knee then to the line where that soft skin disappeared under the shadow of the robe.

He dragged his gaze away. Moving forward meant letting her into his life in a real way. Not telling her everything risked her wrath.

He was torn and frustrated. He was also on fire for her.

Without thinking he reached over and slipped his hand under her ankles. Picked up her feet and put them on his lap, slippers and all. "You must be exhausted."

The move knocked her off-balance, but only for a second. Her hands went to the cushions on either side of her to steady herself. "I'm still on a bit of an adrenaline high."

That made two of them and Derrick didn't see the rush dying any time soon. "Interesting."

His palm skimmed up her leg from her ankle. He massaged first one calf then the other, with his thumb tracing gentle circles over her skin.

Her fingers flexed against the couch material. "Derrick Jameson, are you flirting with me?"

"I'm trying."

Heat flared in her eyes. "That's dangerous."

He'd skated way past that point. For him there was no longer an *if*. It was all about *when*. And if she showed any sign of agreeing, he'd have their clothes off in record time. "No, dangerous is what I *want* to do to you."

She didn't move. "Tell me."

He said goodbye to the idea of getting any work done today. "Any chance you'd let me show you?"

Her gaze went to the floor then to the boxes leaning against the end of the couch. "There's not much room in here."

"My bedroom is pretty spacious." Not his most subtle line, but it was out there now. "Unless you dumped boxes up there, as well."

"I was tempted, but now I'm happy I didn't."

His hand stilled on her calf. "Be sure, Ellie."

"The answer is yes, Derrick."

She didn't know how they made it upstairs without breaking something. The barriers she'd erected, the promises she'd made to herself about not getting involved and the need to ignore her attraction to him... it all floated away.

This was for her. For the first in a long time, she took something she needed and ignored all the sensible reasons to hold back. There, with him, she didn't want to be rational and careful. She wanted heat and passion. Touching and kissing.

She'd stripped his suit jacket off him before they'd gotten out of the living room. She'd had his tie unknotted and slipped off by the time they'd hit the bottom step of the staircase curving up to the second floor.

His footsteps thudded on the stairs as he walked backward, his hand curled around the banister.

He stopped when she dropped the robe. His chest rose and fell on heavy breaths as he stared at her. He didn't touch her, but his gaze traveled over her like a gentle caress.

Never breaking eye contact, he drew her closer, moving her to the step above him. Let his gaze dip to her stomach...to the tops of her legs. The anticipation burned through her. Labored breathing echoed in her ears, a mix of hers and his.

When he grabbed the back of her thighs and pulled her tight against him, her breath escaped her lungs with a hard punch. The next minute he lifted her off her feet. Without any thought from her brain, she wrapped her legs and arms around his firm body. Held him close.

Her fingers slipped into his hair. She loved the feel and smell of him. His strength. His determination.

She lowered her head and kissed him. Poured every ounce of need and want into it, and felt his arms tighten around her in response.

Boy, the man could kiss.

"Damn." He whispered the word when he finally lifted his head. Then he started moving.

There was something breathtakingly sexy about having Derrick carry her up the stairs. About the way his fingers clenched and unclenched against the bare skin on her thighs. He didn't break a sweat.

Their relationship had a ticking clock. For once, she didn't hear it thumping in her head, threatening to steal him out of her life.

The house whirled until everything blurred. At the top of the stairs they passed a doorway, then another. She saw a bed and, in another room, what looked like a desk and a wall of bookcases.

None of it stopped him. Derrick kept walking until they got to the shadowed room at the end of the hall. He hit the light switch with his elbow. A soft light bathed the room in white.

She could see the deep blue walls and closed curtains. So soothing. A huge bed sat smack in the middle of the room with pillows stacked against the head-board. It dominated the space.

The furniture was sleek. Clean lines that hinted at a big price tag. Dark and mysterious…perfect for him.

"Are you sure?"

His question, asked in a deep, even voice, broke through her gawking. She looked at him again. Saw the warmth in his eyes, felt the need vibrating through him. There was only one answer. "Yes."

His hold loosened and she slid down the front of him, felt every inch of his excitement. As soon as her feet hit the floor, her hands went to his chest and she started unbuttoning his shirt. Once she got it open and untucked, he captured her mouth in a kiss that made her knees buckle.

He caught her around the waist and held her with one hand while his other tunneled under her shirt. Then both of his hands were on her, caressing her breasts, learning her curves.

Tension ripped through her. The soft cotton of her shirt suddenly scratched against her. She wanted it up and off. As if she'd said the words out loud, he peeled the shirt up, lifting it off her, leaving her exposed to his gaze.

His thumbs rubbed over her as he cupped her. That intense gaze stayed locked on her breasts, on how they fit his hands. "Ellie…"

He barely touched her and her skin caught on fire. Every nerve ending snapped to life. Every instinct told her to hold him again.

He sat on the edge of the bed and she wanted to slip onto his lap, but he held her between his legs. Had her stand there as he spread his hand over her stomach…

as he slid his fingertips under the band of shorts. With a tug, he had them skimming her body to the tops of her thighs. Wriggling her hips, she shimmied them the rest of the way off.

He stared at her white bikini bottoms. She knew they were see-through. She knew how much she wanted them off.

She climbed on him then. Straddled his lap and pressed her body against his. The way he inhaled, sharp almost as if on a gasp, empowered her. She loved the sound and his loss of control. When he fell onto the mattress, she went with him. They tumbled down and he shifted up on one elbow until he hovered over her.

He trailed his fingers over her stomach to the top of the bikini bottoms.

"You still have a lot of clothes on, big guy."

"I can be naked in two seconds." His palm flattened over the front of her underwear.

She could feel her body getting ready for him. Something inside her tightened and a tumbling started deep in her stomach. "Let's see."

For a second he didn't move. Then his eyebrow lifted. "Anything you want."

He sat up next to her and did a slow striptease, taking his time unbuttoning his dress shirt and sleeves before shucking it off. She couldn't really see anything but the firm muscles of his chest. She wanted to reach up and trail her fingers over that sexy dip between his collarbone and his shoulder. Over every pronounced angle.

"How does a man who spends all of his day at a desk look like you?"

"I don't spend *every* hour there." He winked at her then stood.

His hands went to his belt and that got her moving. She shifted to the side of the bed and dropped her legs over the side. Fit her hands over his and took over the task of undoing his belt. Slid the leather out of the loops and dropped it to the floor.

Next came the zipper. The ripping sound echoed through the room as she lowered it and pressed her palm against his bulge filling the space. Caressed him through his pants.

His fingers tightened against the side of her head. "Ellie, I'm not going to last very much longer."

"Good." She slid her legs beneath her and moved back. Lay against the mattress with her feet flat on the bed and her knees in the air.

He visibly swallowed. She watched him do it. Smiled when he nearly ripped his pants and boxer briefs getting them off. Then he was naked and so fit, so lean and sexy, as he crawled up the mattress to get to her.

That fast her heart flipped over. A revving sensation took off inside her. She slid her leg up the back of his, loving the burst of energy that flowed through her at the touch.

She wanted this. Him. That first time she'd seen him in person the air had left her lungs. Seeped out until she couldn't breathe. Every time since, her heartbeat did a little dance. His face, his body, even his grouchy personality combined in one intriguing package that she itched to open.

They had weeks left on the agreement and a need to make it look real. For whatever time they had left, she would. She'd put aside the worries and the ways it could go wrong and would dive in. And then she'd somehow walk away from him.

Right as he dipped his head to kiss her again he froze. "Damn."

She grabbed on to his upper arms. "What is it?"

The sound coming from him could only be described as a growl. "I bought condoms but I left them at work."

For some reason that made her laugh. "Did you think we were going to have sex on your desk?"

"It is a reoccurring fantasy of mine." He lifted up, just a fraction, and looked down her body. "But I can still touch you. Give you what you need."

Before she could say anything or even put a sentence together, his fingers slipped into her underwear. He skimmed his hand between her legs, over her. Gentle yet demanding. When one finger slid inside her, her breath caught in her throat.

His tongue swept over her nipple in a long lick that left her shaking. Sensations bombarded her from all directions. The mix of touching and tasting had her lower back lifting off the bed. When he did it again, all the air sucked out of her.

She felt light and dizzy and so ready for him. Her fingernails dug into his shoulders to hold him close. "Derrick, yes."

He pumped his finger inside her, bringing her body to snapping attention. Every intelligent thought left her head, leaving only one lingering fact. "I have an IUD."

His head shot up. "What?"

"Birth control."

His mouth dropped open before he said anything. "I got tested."

Now it was her turn to be confused. "I don't…"

"I have a report for you to see. You know, just in case. Not sure why I forgot the condoms."

His finger stayed inside her during the surreal and very not sexy conversation. But it was practical and smart…and it pushed out thoughts of risk and most of her common sense.

She slipped her hand down his body, between them, and circled his length. Her palm slid against him from base to tip.

"Ellie, please be sure." He shook his head. "We can wait if you—"

His words cut off when she wrapped her fingers around him and squeezed. "Now, Derrick."

Light flashed in his eyes as he nodded. Then he was on his knees between her legs. Her body hummed as he peeled her underwear off. Pushing her legs apart, he settled between them. His tongue replaced his fingers and excitement surged inside her.

Her heels dug into the mattress and she twisted the comforter in her balled hands as his mouth worked its magic. When he hit the right spot, her thighs pressed against his shoulders. A moan trapped in her throat begged to escape.

She shifted and twisted as the pleasure threatened to overtake her. Still, he didn't stop his sensual caress. That tongue. Those fingers. Every part of him, from the heat of his mouth to the expert use of his hands, had her straining to hold back as her body bucked.

Right as she hovered on the edge, he got to his knees. He was hard and ready and he didn't wait. She lost her breath as he pushed inside her, filling her. Her breath hiccupped as her inner muscles tightened around him. When he pulled out and pushed in again, she grabbed him and brought him closer.

He leaned over and his chest pressed against her. Heat pounded off his skin and a thin sheen of sweat appeared along his shoulders. She held on to him, traced a line of kisses up his throat.

Their bodies moved as he plunged in and out. The pressure built as she fought her release. She ached to make it last but Derrick's muscles began to shake. When he slipped his hand between their bodies and touched her again, her control broke.

The winding inside her shattered and her body let go. She rode out the pulses and pleasure, gasping as his head fell to her shoulder. She could hear the uptake in his breathing and feel the muscles across his back stiffen. She caressed and kissed him as he came. When his body finally stopped moving, he balanced against her. The weight made her feel warm and secure. Happy even.

After a few seconds he turned his head to the side and his breath blew across her neck. "That was pretty great."

Her fingers lingered in his damp hair. "It was the slippers. They're sexy."

She burst out laughing first, then he joined her. It took them almost a full minute to stop. But they didn't move for a lot longer. What scared her was she didn't want to. She was content to stay there forever.

Ten

The DC Insider: *It looks like we may need to find a new Hottest Ticket in Town. Derrick Jameson and Ellie Gold have been living it up. Dates and dinners. There's even a rumor that they'll be attending a charity event together next week. Does this mean Derrick plans to put a ring on it? We'll have to wait and see.*

Derrick knew he was in trouble the second he opened his office door. Both Spence and Jackson were in there. Spence looked at home in the big chair with his feet up on the desk. A bit too comfortable, but at least he was in the office, which was more than he'd been in months.

Spence made a show of looking at his watch. "You were gone for two hours."

Yeah, that was the last thing Derrick intended to talk about. "I had something I needed to do."

Truth was the sex had him reeling. He hadn't even used protection. That had never happened in his adult life. He'd never even been tempted to skip that step. With Ellie, he wanted it all. He ignored the risks.

The idea of a fake arrangement had backfired on him. He didn't want an on-paper-only relationship with Ellie. Then again, he didn't know *what* he wanted with her. Nothing made sense, including his choices, at the moment.

"How is Ellie adjusting to her new house?" Jackson asked.

Her house. Just the thought of that should have set off an explosion in Derrick's brain. He was not a guy to settle down. He rarely invited women to his house. That's what hotels were for.

He maintained a strict wall, keeping almost everyone but a select few out of his most personal space. But with Ellie the lines had blurred from the very start.

"She was less than impressed that I went ahead and scheduled the movers." Talk about an understatement.

"Women." Spence shook his head. "Man, you'd think they'd love having their stuff packed up without telling them first."

Derrick glared at Jackson. "You told him."

"It was too good not to share," Jackson said, not even bothering to deny it.

Spence leaned back with his arms folded behind his head. "Big brother, can I give you some advice?"

That wasn't what Derrick wanted right now. "Get up first."

Spence whistled. "You're grumpy for a guy who had sex. You did, right? I hate to think you look that disheveled just from talking."

"I was fine until I walked in here." That was pretty much all Derrick wanted to say on that topic, so he gestured for Spence to get up then took his seat.

"The advice?" Spence leaned on the edge of Derrick's desk.

"Right. From the guy who isn't dating anyone." Derrick held out a hand. "Please enlighten me."

"I talked with Ellie for fifteen minutes and I think you need to be careful."

That got Derrick's attention. "Of her?"

"Of losing her, dumb-ass. Don't mess this up."

Not bad brotherly advice. "I'm trying not to."

Spence shook his head. "Try harder."

The day had been this whirlwind of emotions. As soon as Derrick left the house to go back to work—because *of course he did*—panic set in. She worried about what would happen when he came home and what they'd say to each other tonight. The whole thing was now awkward and weird.

Planning the rest of the day after surprise sex was not easy. So, Ellie relied on the same thing she always did—Vanessa. She moved around Derrick's chef-caliber kitchen right now, cutting vegetables and making a salad.

Vanessa was there, just in case. Kind of like a shield against bumbling conversation. How Derrick would feel about guests in his house was a different question, one Ellie hadn't thought about until right now as she heard footsteps on the stairs. Well, if he didn't like it, that would teach him to move her in without talking to her first.

Ellie plastered on a smile as soon as she saw him. "You're home."

His gaze hesitated on her face before skipping to the counter and the stack of cutting boards and knives sitting there. "You're cooking?"

"Don't sound so surprised." Sure, it was fair, but still.

Vanessa popped her head around the corner. "Also, don't panic. I'm helping."

Derrick gave Vanessa a small wave as he stopped beside Ellie. "You can't cook?"

She snorted. "Can you?"

"I can grill. Men grill."

Vanessa winced. "Oh, boy."

"Typical," Ellie said at the same time. "Well, if you're done impressing us with your testosterone... Derrick, this is Vanessa, my best friend." She rushed to add one caveat. "The one person other than Jackson who knows this—us—isn't real."

His expression went blank. "It's not?"

"The contract thing." For some reason it hurt to say the words this time.

It's not as if they had some sort of miracle sex. It was great and her body still hummed, but she didn't think sex solved everything. Though she had to admit, something did change. Inside her, deep inside.

Together they were sexy and comfortable...they worked. The churning, that ramped-up feeling of being excited to see him and to hear his voice, didn't strike her as fake. She'd never experienced it before and it made her a little twitchy now because she hadn't had enough time to analyze it, but she knew it amounted to more than a practical agreement between friends.

She had such a short time to savor this feeling. She'd been the one who insisted on limiting the time of the agreement to two months. He had wanted more months and now she did, too.

Derrick still didn't show any reaction. His affect had gone flat and stayed there. "You told her."

She rewound the comment in her head, looking for any judgment, but didn't hear it. That didn't mean it wasn't there. "Is that a problem?"

For a second he just stood there, not talking. Then a lightness stole over him and he glanced at Vanessa. "You don't have a habit of gossiping or talking to the *Insider*, do you?"

The hint of amusement calmed Ellie. Her neck muscles unclenched as she relaxed again.

"Any secret Ellie tells me stays with me," Vanessa said.

"Happy to hear it." Derrick stopped in front of the lasagna pan and put his finger out as if he intended to poke it. "So, what's this—?"

"Stop." Ellie slapped his hand away. "You have to wait."

He smiled at her. "Should I order takeout to be safe?"

That look… His walls fell and he stopped being the commanding-man-in-charge-of-everything to be a man. This was at-home Derrick and she had no defense against this sexy side of him. This was the Derrick who had landed her in his bed—and would put her back there. This Derrick was dangerous.

But that didn't mean that she was ready to let him off the hook for his behavior earlier. Her arms still ached from the quick move she and Vanessa had made of most of her stuff to one of the extra bedrooms upstairs.

Oh, no. He'd be paying for that one for a while. "Tough talk from a guy who made a big mistake today."

Vanessa turned around, spoon in hand. "Yeah, you owe me for carrying all those books around."

"Technically, that's Ellie's fault since I hired movers. She sent them away," Derrick said.

Vanessa shook the long spoon at him. "I heard you were Mr. Bossy Pants."

Derrick groaned as he made his way around the counter and took a seat on one of the bar stools. "Oh, good. Now I get to fight two of you."

The byplay made Ellie smile. She hadn't been raised with banter in the kitchen. Her entire childhood had raged like a house on fire. There was always some new crisis and not enough money to handle it.

There were no settled moments of her parents joking with each other, or very few of them. Stealing a few now with Derrick had a warmth settling deep inside her. She'd always wanted this—a home and security. Someone who made her hot but also made her want to snuggle on the couch.

"Are we wrong?" she asked, wanting the moment to continue for just a bit longer.

"No." He rested his hands on the counter. "Today I was an overbearing jackass."

Ellie almost dropped the glass she'd picked up. "Whoa?"

Vanessa looked from Derrick to Ellie. "What?"

"What you heard was progress."

"I can learn." He shrugged as he stole a mushroom off the salad and popped it in his mouth.

Ellie wanted to believe that. She was desperate to believe that and she wasn't even sure why. "But can you set the table?"

He winked at her. "I'm on it."

She watched him meander around the kitchen. He rolled up his shirtsleeves and dug in. Grabbed the plates and silverware. Even hummed while he did it, which Ellie found oddly endearing.

And the man could move. Those long, determined strides. The long legs and that flat stomach. She'd seen him without his clothes and with them on, and she was a fan of both.

She glanced at the table. "Three? Isn't Spence coming home?"

"He's having dinner with Jackson. There was some thought tonight might be loud around here." Derrick shot her a sexy little smile. "From all the yelling, which Spence thinks I deserve."

"I like him."

"Yeah, I figured you would." Derrick finished with the table and walked back to the counter.

Ellie expected him to stand there or look at his watch, or even try to fit in a half hour of work before dinner. Instead he draped an arm loosely over her shoulder and brought her in close to his side.

Vanessa did a double take but didn't say anything.

"So, what else can I do?" he asked.

As far as Ellie was concerned, he was doing it.

* * *

Hours later dinner was over and the dishes were done and put away. Vanessa hung around, telling stories about the men they'd dated and some of their stranger travel adventures. To Derrick's credit, he listened and asked questions. He genuinely seemed to enjoy the night even though Ellie guessed he'd rather be tied to his desk working.

Now it was almost midnight. Vanessa had gone and Spence had come home. After a bit of small talk, he'd settled into the bedroom he always used when he was in town. Ellie started the night in Derrick's bedroom because it would have been weird for them to sleep separately if they were really dating.

Some of her clothes, the ones she and Vanessa managed to collect before dinner, hung in Derrick's oversize closet. The thing was as big as two rooms with shelves and racks and drawers and a chair.

A chair.

When the house went quiet, she'd snuck to the bedroom she intended to sleep in even though she wanted to stay with him, wanted to forget that Spence slept nearby and that stupid agreement. She craved his touch. Needed him to hold her, kiss her, roll around in that big bed with her.

She wasn't really the casual sex type. She needed a connection, a relationship. She didn't have a lot of experience but all of it included condoms.

So much had happened over the last few months. She couldn't even process it all. Her nerves were frazzled. A list of pros and cons kept cycling through her head.

With Derrick everything was different. More intense. Less clear. She'd bent her personal rules until they broke. Instead of feeling guilty or thinking she'd messed up, a wave of sadness hit her. A sense of loss at not being with him now. Of not being able to hold him, to touch him tonight, like she'd thought about all day.

She thought back to the first time he'd proposed this fake arrangement. The whole thing had confused and annoyed her, but something in his eyes and voice had compelled her. She'd agreed to an arrangement she'd never go for under any other circumstance.

Sure, there was the Noah piece. The part about her needing money and some bit of security. All that was real, but the truth was she'd signed that agreement because she'd *wanted* to. Because, for once, she took something she wanted—Derrick.

For the first time in her life she operated without a road map. She let emotion guide her. She saw the risks and accepted them, even knowing that the likelihood was this would end in pain and heartache. There really was no other way for a relationship built on fake facts to finish.

She was so lost in thought she almost missed the soft knock on the door. When it sounded the second time, she scooted out of bed, careful to make sure her shorts and T-shirt were in place when she opened the door in case the visitor was Spence.

Derrick stood there in what looked like lounge pants and a gray T-shirt that fit him like a second skin. That fast, her temperature spiked and her insides started to whirl.

She gripped the side of the door. "Are you okay?"

They'd worked out this plan about getting up early and keeping her bed made and door shut. Derrick had talked about using the excuse of her stacking her stuff in here until she could go through it all. She was accustomed to living with boxes, so having them around now didn't bother her.

"I wanted to check on you." Derrick shifted his weight from foot to foot.

The move struck her as uncharacteristic and a bit vulnerable. "I don't—"

"May I come in?"

Good grief, it was his house. She stepped back. "Of course."

He walked in and caught her up in his arms. His mouth covered hers in a kiss that had her forgetting about boxes and clothes and just about everything else. She grabbed his shoulders, dug in and held him close as pleasure pulsed through her. When he lifted his head a few seconds later, she felt breathless and weak. Her resolve had melted along with her resistance.

"I've wanted to do that since I got home from work," he said in a whisper against her lips.

Tonight had been incredibly special. She'd laughed until she couldn't breathe. She'd built memories. Discovered a warmth she'd never known growing up because everything had been so uncertain between her father's and Noah's moods.

She trusted and loved Vanessa. She was an integral part of Ellie's life. Derrick was supposed to be temporary, but her feelings for him, how she thought about him during the day, were anything but fake. They'd started this ruse by barely talking and now she texted him every day. Sometimes she made up silly things to ask, just to see his response. And he always responded.

"We are inviting trouble." She said it more to convince herself than him.

"I know." Derrick rested his forehead against hers. "I guess I can't convince you to join me in my bedroom?"

He could, so easily. That was the problem. "We should…"

"Right." He gave her arms a gentle squeeze then dropped his hands.

She felt the loss to her bones. It settled in and had her trembling. But she couldn't go overboard with her feelings. "Derrick."

"I'll let you get some sleep." He kissed her on the forehead, quick and simple.

Then he was gone and it was all she could do to keep from calling him back.

Eleven

The DC Insider: *We're hearing there are a few snags in the Derrick and Ellie forever plan. Her baby brother refuses to stay quiet. Her past continues to be a problem. And is our Hottest Ticket in Town having second thoughts about a serious relationship?*

Two days later Derrick sent Noah a message from Ellie's phone, asking him to meet her at her old apartment. This was the last day before she turned the keys over. Noah didn't know that, but Derrick did. He hoped that excused him sneaking her phone while she'd gone upstairs to shower this morning after their coffee together.

They'd done that for the past two days. No more sex, despite his attempts to make it happen. But she was holding back and having Spence hanging around turned out to be a bit of a mood killer. So did the calls from their father. All of a sudden he had work questions again, and that made Derrick nervous.

Through it all, she wandered around in her pajamas each morning. If that's how people acted when they lived together in a real relationship, Derrick kind of got it. There was something energizing about spending those fifteen minutes with her in the morning before he took off.

She didn't have to get up when he did or to fumble her way downstairs like she had this morning when she'd looked half-asleep and almost missed the bottom step. The coffee time didn't have to happen to prolong the ploy for Spence because he was still asleep at that time of the morning. That meant she did it for him, and that thrilled Derrick more than he wanted it to.

The door opened behind him and Noah stormed inside. He took a few steps then stopped. "Where is my sister?"

He sounded more concerned than angry, which may have saved him from the full-scale ass-kicking Derrick wanted to unleash. But they still had issues, and Derrick had promised Ellie he'd put those to bed, so he tried one more time. "We need to talk."

"Her stuff is gone from her apartment." Noah still frowned as he turned around in a circle in the middle of the room. "Her couch and her—"

"Noah, stop." He seemed locked in some sort of shock. "I called you here."

"But she's—"

"Living with me."

That got Noah's attention. He stopped moving and stared at Derrick. "You can't be serious."

"I am."

That familiar red flush of anger spread over Noah's face. "Nothing is off-limits with you."

The comment hit harder than Derrick expected. He felt the shot right to his gut. When it came to Ellie, he had crossed a bunch of lines, most Noah didn't even know about, but Derrick couldn't pretend he hadn't backed her into a corner and used her love for her brother against her.

He had to deal with that. Take it apart and assess it because now that he did, it seemed like an Eldrick Jameson move. Something his father would do to ensure he got his way. Derrick didn't like that comparison one bit.

"There aren't any cameras or videos in here. You don't need to pretend we had a confrontation at work. You can drop the bullshit." Derrick had to accept his part in a lot of sins where the Gold family was concerned, but not that one.

"I didn't steal anything."

"Noah, come on." Derrick didn't know how the guy could stand there and lie. How he could actually frown, curl his shoulders in and look like the injured party.

Derrick had taken a chance on him. They met when a friend from high school, now a college professor, called Derrick about a kid he found sneaking around the computer labs at George Washington University. The kid—Noah—had created a student ID and had been using university resources to play games and check out the internal supposedly confidential workings of the school.

Noah hadn't had the experience or the college requirements for the job he'd held at Derrick's company. But like the professor, Derrick had seen something in Noah. A need to prove himself. The brilliance waiting to be tapped. He'd given him a chance and brought him on. Thought of him as a mentee of sorts…then he'd stolen from the company and tried to turn Derrick's life upside down.

Noah shook his head. "You don't get it."

Something in his words and that tone got to Derrick. The sentence he was about to say died in his head. Now he wanted to know what was happening in Noah's head. "Explain it to me."

Noah went to the window and looked out. "I found out about you."

Other than the agreement with Ellie and his father's stipulations, Derrick didn't have much to hide. There were things he wished people didn't know, but he never had that luxury. "Noah, I hate to break this to you but my life is not exactly a big secret. I've had the press on me since I was in elementary school."

Thanks to his family, starting with his politician grandfather, the family got in the news and stayed there. Derrick started dating and the cameras were there to capture his young bachelor days. When they broke up, the girl's family sold a story about him to the tabloids.

The only time he ever got behind the wheel after drinking, the dumbest thing he'd ever done, the press had shown up then, too. He'd learned a harsh lesson that time, and many others.

His mistakes played out in public. His father excused them before the cameras and berated him behind the scenes. That's how it worked in the Jameson household.

"Did you cheat then, too?" Noah asked as he turned around to face Derrick.

Derrick's mind went blank. "What?"

"Abby."

There was an Abby who worked for him. She had a history with the Jameson men, but not him. He searched his mind for another woman with that name. Any woman named anything close. "Abby who?"

"My sister is going to find out who you really are." Noah nodded. All traces of uncertainty had disappeared. "She will. The people at the *Insider* will."

"Have you been talking with them, Noah?" If he'd planted that story about Ellie and her former job, his blood relationship to her would not save him. Derrick would move in and set him straight.

Noah shrugged. "What if I have?"

It took every ounce of willpower Derrick possessed to tamp down on his anger. "Do not ruin your sister's reputation."

"Me?"

Derrick tried reason one more time. "You stole from me and I caught you. You're trying to blow this up into something else and hurt Ellie, and I'm not sure why."

"Did you lead Abby on, too? Make her promises and then dump her?"

"What are you talking about?"

"I know what it's like to be one of your chosen few then get kicked aside." Noah was yelling now, but there was an underlying thread, an edge that suggested he'd been hurt.

The words crashed through Derrick. "Is that what this is really about? Because that did not happen."

"I'm leaving." Noah headed for the door.

Everything was so unsettled, maybe even worse than before they'd talked. Derrick wasn't sure what to say because nothing Noah mentioned made any sense to him. "You've got to stop, Noah. I don't want to hurt you and I certainly don't want Ellie hurt."

"This is your fault." Noah shook his head then slipped into the hallway, but not before taking one final shot. "You'll see."

It had been three days since they'd had sex. Every night they'd pretend to go into his bedroom together then she'd sneak out. Inevitably, about fifteen minutes later there would be a knock on the door. Derrick saying good-night. Derrick kissing her. Last night, Derrick tunneling his hands up her shirt and touching her, which she'd absolutely encouraged.

But when he showed an interest in more, she pulled back. She had to until she could get her thoughts in order. Being there, the domesticity, it all felt real. The first time together had been all consuming. She wanted to act like she could handle a no-strings fake relationship and walk away, but she wasn't sure.

She waited for those before-bed visits. Yearned for them with a fierceness that scared her. Last night she sat on her bed, staring at the doorknob, willing it to turn. It took him a full eighteen minutes to show up. She'd spent every one of those extra seconds counting down, trying to drown out the doubts welling inside her and making her jumpy.

That sort of unsettled sensation couldn't be normal. It had her reassessing, even as she knew she'd give in. Because she wanted to give in. She wanted more from him, for them…and that was the problem.

Now, they were out in public. All dressed up, with him in a tux that looked like he'd been born to wear. The black coat with his nearly black hair…she'd actually made a small *pfffing* sound when he'd come out of the bedroom. No one should look that good. Ever.

When Derrick mentioned a charity gala a few days ago, she'd told him she planned to be sick that day. Gala sounded like an opportunity for more cameras and she was about done with that part of their arrangement. He responded by threatening to drag her to it in her gym shorts, which left her no choice but to borrow a fancy dress from Vanessa. Thank goodness for those money-raising gallery events Vanessa hosted all the time.

The gown was beautiful in a princess sort of way. It had a fitted sleeveless top covered with beads and a long, flowing, light blue skirt in a fabric soft enough to beat out those expensive sheets Derrick had at the house. Vanessa was taller, so Ellie had on three-inch heels she was pretty sure would snap her ankle in two if she stepped the wrong way.

Vanessa also wore a smaller bra size, so the top of the dress, while stunning and sparkly, was also slowly strangling Ellie. She put her hand on her stomach and tried to figure out how to permanently suck it in. "I think I'm going to pop."

Derrick looked over at her. His gaze slipped to her

hand, which had moved to her chest. "I have no idea what to say to that."

"The bodice on this is a bit tight." It was choking her. But why be dramatic about it? "It has to be to hold everything in, but wow."

His gaze shifted to the tops of her breasts, which were spilling out more than they probably should be. "Well, we wouldn't want anything sliding out."

"It's Vanessa's fault. My boobs are bigger." She touched them as if she needed to emphasize the point.

"Okay, yeah. I'm purposely not going to talk about your best friend's body."

Ellie couldn't help but smile at that. He looked on the defensive and a little haunted by the idea. "Good call."

"I'm not a total dumb-ass." He took a sip of his champagne as he glanced at the dance floor.

A few couples moved around, looking stiff and out of place. Between this event and the one where she'd met Derrick, Ellie had come up with a theory. Many DC business people didn't exactly thrive in social situations.

Derrick looked perfectly suited to the room. Just as he looked great behind his desk and adorable in the morning in his lounge pants as he sipped his coffee in the kitchen. She'd never met anyone who "fit" into any situation like he did before.

"You are such a guy." The comment slipped out before she could think it through.

Derrick being Derrick, he did not let it slide by him. "I'm going to regret this but…what?"

"You look like *that*." She waved a hand over him, up and down as she took in every perfect inch. "You probably get up looking like that."

He followed her gaze. "I don't generally wear the tux to bed."

"Well, you should. You look ridiculously hot." When his eyebrow lifted and his attention switched from half scanning the room to full force on her, she snorted. "Oh, please. Don't look surprised. You own a mirror. I'm sure there will be a thousand photos of us all over the internet tomorrow and you can see for yourself."

She hoped her too-tight dress photographed okay. It would suck to stand next to him, looking all Hottest Ticket in Town, and her coming off as someone who snuck her way into the photo.

He put his mostly full glass on the tray held by a passing server. "If that's what it takes to get you in my bedroom, I will wear the tux all the time at home. Honestly, the going-to-bed-alone thing sucks."

She thought so, too. She also knew it was over. With him looking at her like that and her willpower gone, it was inevitable.

"Shh. There are ears everywhere." No one stared at them after his comment. Well, no one other than the ones already staring. Derrick did attract attention. "And cameras."

"Don't blame me this time. The charity hired them."

His hand brushed against hers. She didn't realize what was happening until his warm fingers slid through hers. Hand holding. It was so innocent and sweet...she almost jumped him right there.

"What about the photographer who followed me home from the coffee place today?" The guy had stepped right in front of her. One second sooner and she would have thrown her coffee at him on instinct. "I had barely brushed my hair."

He lifted their joined hands and kissed the back of hers. "You look beautiful."

She was pretty sure she saw a camera bulb flash but she tried to ignore it. "I didn't then."

"I bet you did."

They stood in a room full of people and he made her feel like the only other person in the room. He had that gift. For a man who commanded his way through life, issuing orders, he didn't seem to get that just being there, looking like that, was enough to get people's attention.

A sudden case of nerves shot through her. She was out of her comfort zone and out with him, a man she'd started to dream about. People watched. Others whispered. Tomorrow every movement would be analyzed and dissected online.

It overwhelmed her, stole her breath. She rushed to find a non-Derrick thing to talk about. "My father would have loved this."

"He enjoyed parties?"

They still held hands and when she didn't answer right away, Derrick gave her fingers a gentle squeeze. That only confused her more. "Do you really not know?"

His smile lit up his face. "This cryptic thing you do is oddly endearing but it does confuse the hell out of me sometimes."

She refused to be sucked in by that sexy look. Talking about a harsh reality suddenly seemed easier than dealing with her growing and confusing feelings for Derrick. "My dad. He was *that* guy. The one who always had this big plan to make money. He met a man with a great idea here. He had a lead on something big there."

"Did anything ever pan out?" Derrick asked.

"No." She tried to remember a clear success and couldn't come up with one. "My entire childhood is filled with memories of him spending the last dollar on this dream or using the money for the electric bill to invest in some weird scheme."

She knew that sounded harsh. Maybe it was too much, but all she had was her perspective and the reality of moving around and never feeling secure.

"What about your mom?"

"She enabled it. I mean, she tried to talk to him. So much time was spent on dad's needs that I think maybe Noah's issues got overlooked." The pieces came together in her head. She'd tried for so long to keep it all separate but it did connect. Because of how her parents lived their lives, Ellie got stuck in a parental role that made her more sarcastic and less trusting. "I would hear her…"

Maybe that was enough of that. Ellie tried to concentrate on the music and the laughter floating through the room. To escape reality for a second.

"What?" he asked.

Derrick's gentle tone coaxed her on. "Crying."

"Ellie, I'm sorry." He slid his arm around her and pulled her closer.

"He always thought there was something better out there, you know. That if he could put the deals together the right way, he'd hit it big." No one could deliver the line like her dad. He had believed, or he'd sounded like he did. "He never understood that we didn't care about that. They died going to one last big event."

For a few seconds Derrick didn't say anything. He kept that reassuring hand on her lower back and they swayed to the music. People moved around them. A few stopped to say hello but didn't linger. They must have projected the couple-in-love vibe because most people just seemed to smile at them.

"It's possible he thought it was his job. You know, to make the family financially secure." Derrick made the comment without looking at her. He focused on a table of businessmen instead.

She saw Joe Cantor in the group. That explained Derrick's sudden interest. Since she didn't want another scene, she responded when she might otherwise have let it slip past her. "But he did the opposite."

Derrick glanced at her then. "That, I get."

"The rich boy understands being poor?" She tried to keep her voice light. Tried and failed. She regretted lashing out as soon as she did it. "Sorry. I didn't mean to take that shot."

"It's okay." He nodded toward the couples milling near them. "Dance?"

"Derrick." She reached for his hand and managed to snag it.

"We should dance, Ellie." With that, he pulled her into his arms and maneuvered them to the edge of the dance floor. After a few minutes the stiffness in his shoulders eased and the distance between them closed. Her body rested against his. The scent of his shampoo filled her senses.

She forgot about their conversation and the people watching them. The public ruse fell away until it was just the two of them—a man and a woman swaying on the dance floor. Holding each other, wrapped around each other.

She looked up and stared at his chin, those lips. "Derrick…"

"Keep that up and we're going to need to leave early." His voice sounded rough and lower than usual.

Feminine power surged through her. "Good."

The dance did it. He'd respected her boundaries and would keep doing so, but the dance brought her walls crashing down. He felt it as soon as it happened. Saw it in her eyes as she looked up at him.

He made a mental note to dance with her more often.

But that would come later. After all that touching he couldn't get them home fast enough. After the meal and the silent auction, both of which felt as if they lasted five lifetimes, he suggested they go. They'd said their goodbyes and scrambled for the door. He didn't think anyone noticed. The diced-up feeling came from inside him. He tried to hide it. They had that damn agreement to uphold, after all.

He stepped into the kitchen and dropped his tux jacket over the couch. His plan was to linger for a second, enough not to be rude, then head upstairs.

He got as far as the couch before Ellie started talking. "Have you forgiven me?"

He glanced over his shoulder, not really focusing on her during his quick look. Call it self-preservation. "What are you talking about?"

"I was a jerk tonight."

He hadn't expected that. Debating whether he should let it drop, he turned around to face her. "That's quite an admission."

"Derrick, I'm serious."

She stood there in a dress that showed off her curves and lit her face. It had taken all of his strength to resist her tonight. When she'd first come downstairs in that, he'd wanted to skip the public event that would help shore up their arrangement and drag her right up to bed. The temptation still punched at him.

He remembered her shot about being poor. She clearly thought that was the only problem that could happen to a family. "My family isn't a good subject for me."

He didn't know where that came from or why he said it. Well, he knew *why* but not *why now*.

"They're part of you. Your dad, your upbringing. It's all a piece of who you are."

She didn't know but that was the absolute worst thing she could have said. "I sure as hell hope not."

Her head shot back. "I don't get it."

How did he explain? Did he even want to? Every slight and every fault piled up over the years. He knew he had it easy compared to others. This wasn't a race but he hadn't exactly had a smooth time, either.

Some of that had changed with his father's new wife, Jackie. Or so people said. Derrick didn't spend much time with his father since he'd been the one to suggest his father think about retiring. He and Jackie had been living on an island, racing through money ever since.

"You guessed before that my dad was difficult. He's a… I can't even think of a nice way to put it. An ass?" His father wasn't a great man. He hurt women. A lot of women. He treated them like property. He'd ruined their mother's life. He acted as if his employees and friends were expendable. He saw his sons as disappointing playthings to bring out for photo ops but little else. "He ran through women, never quite finishing with one before moving on to the other. He sucked with money."

"Your family is…well, aren't you all millionaires, or billionaires or whatever comes after that?" Ellie took a quick look around the house as she spoke.

Derrick got it. He lived a certain way. Not over-the-top or even equal to a lot of other business people in town with his level of success, but he didn't suffer many hardships. But that was all thanks to his hard work, not his father's.

"Both of our fathers had issues with money."

Her eyes widened. "Really?"

"Mine spent money faster than he made it. He was always more impressed with the public version of the family and work than what was happening in private."

She took a few steps and ended up in front of him. "What does that mean?"

"He asked my mother for a divorce while she was dying in a hospital bed." Derrick didn't reach out for Ellie even though he wanted to. The idea of saying those words and touching anyone seemed wrong.

Her mouth twisted in a sour expression. "Who does that?"

"Exactly." She got it. She understood Dad wasn't just the handsome face that appeared in the news now and then. "He spent money and pretended he had an endless supply of it. Meanwhile, he failed to reinvest in the company, retain good employees or expand when times changed."

She reached out first. Her palm flattened against his chest. "But you did. You rebuilt everything."

Derrick exhaled, liking the feel of her skin against his, even through his shirt. He folded his hand over hers. "Me and the people who work for me."

The start of a smile kicked up the corner of her mouth. "You're not going to take credit?"

Not out loud. Not ever. "I've spent my entire life trying not to be him, Ellie. I keep my head down and work. I don't get involved with people."

"Wait, that's not true." Her fingers curled into the material of his shirt as if she were willing him to listen to her. "You and Jackson are close. I sense you're close to your brothers."

"True."

Her second hand slipped to his waist to rest on the top edge of his pants. "You're a good man."

Derrick tried not to think about her fingers or how good they felt on him. "Am I? Your brother hates me and I forced you into a fake relationship."

She threw her hands out to the sides. "Do I look like I don't want to be here?"

The words slammed into him. He wanted her there. Agreement or no, he wanted her in his house, in his bed. In his life. To hell with the emotional consequences. "Then why are we sleeping in separate beds?"

Those hands slipped up his chest to his tie. It loosened a second later. "That's over."

Twelve

The DC Insider: *Dear readers...why are hot millionaire businessmen so hard to read?*

Derrick's hands shook as he lowered the zipper of her dress. Ellie couldn't think of a more satisfying reaction. Couldn't believe how right it felt to be in this bedroom with him. His bedroom.

His fingers brushed over her skin and his hot breath blew against her hair. She held on to the front of the gown, trying to catch it before the whole thing whooshed to the floor. If it were hers she wouldn't care, but it wasn't and that meant being extra careful.

"You're not wearing a bra." Derrick's voice carried a note of awe as he trailed his palm over her back.

Her breath caught and she fought to hold her voice steady. "The dress held everything in."

More like sucked it in and made her skin roll in places she preferred not to have rolls. None of that took away from the specialness of it all. She'd never dreamed about being a princess. She'd let her father do the unrealistic dreaming in the family.

Even with her practical streak, the memory of standing there on Derrick's arm, feeling his strong hand in hers as they'd danced under the lights with her dress swirling around her ran through her mind. She wanted to store away every moment and hold on to how freeing every moment had been.

"Any chance Vanessa has ten or fifteen more like this for you to borrow?" With the zipper the whole way down, Derrick's fingers lingered at the small dip of her lower back. He traced a pattern there.

Her entire body shivered in reaction. Every muscle shook as waves of pleasure ran through her.

She cleared her throat, trying to sound somewhat coherent. "Do we have more fancy events to attend?"

He kissed her bare shoulder. The move relaxed her, lured her in. Then he bit with only the barest of pressure, licked the wound and kissed the spot again. Her pulse took off on a wild race. She could feel it thump in her neck and under his mouth.

That mouth, so perfect, knew just where to nip and how to drive her wild.

He started to trail the kisses up the side of her neck. "I thought you could model them here, in private. With me as your only, but very eager, audience."

He was about to get *so* lucky.

"Aren't you naughty?" She asked the question as she turned in his arms. Seeing his face, running her finger over the stubble on his chin, set off a flurry of activity in her stomach.

On purpose, she let the top of the dress fall to her waist. Only the flare of her hips kept it up at all, and that balance was tenuous at best. She didn't cover herself. Didn't have to. He'd seen every inch of her. Toured his hands and mouth all over her. And when he saw her breasts now, all he could do was stare.

She couldn't imagine a better reaction. His pleasure became her pleasure.

Her feminine power exploded.

"I want to be a bad boy but I'm afraid of tearing the dress."

"Good call." She wiggled her hips and the material fell. She caught it before it hit the floor and handed it to him. "Here."

For a second he stood there with the dress draped over his arm. "Damn."

He wasn't looking at her face. No, his gaze traveled up and down her legs. To her thigh-high stockings with the lacy tops and the matching nude-colored underwear. She'd worn the combination for him.

"You like?" she asked, even though she knew from his expression he did.

"So that you're clear, I like you pretty much any way you'll let me have you." He used his finger to trace the lace pattern on the top of her thigh. "But damn."

Perfect reaction.

He'd stripped his tie off and shrugged out of his jacket. She went to work on his shirt. It took her about two seconds to get those small white buttons undone and to pull back the edges to reveal that firm, tanned chest. "Let's get this off you."

"I can do it." But he didn't make any move to help.

"I'll take care of you." She stripped the shirt off then sat on the edge of the bed.

She skipped the talking and asking and went right to the button at the top of his pants. His breathing kicked up as she lowered the zipper then pushed his dress pants to his knees. The boxer briefs went next.

When she took his length into her hand, his fingers slipped through her hair and held her close. The noise he made when she took him in her mouth, half moan, half yell for joy, sounded like music. It would stay in her head for a long time.

"Ellie." His voice dipped even lower than normal and held an extra-rough edge.

She licked her tongue over his tip then peeked up at him. "I didn't think you'd mind."

"I'm trying to figure out how I've stayed away from you for the past five nights."

"Sheer willpower on both our parts." Wasted time, as far as she was concerned. She wanted this. Wanted him. "To prove we could."

To continue the farce that this was fake and meant nothing…that was over. In reality, what they shared had started to mean everything.

She was falling for him. The words rolled through her head without a signal from her brain. They should have scared her and had her ducking for the toilet. She'd refrained from any real involvement up until now. Found excuses with other boyfriends to cut things off. With Derrick she wanted more, not less.

She understood him. They were good together. He made her rethink some of the views she held and things she took for granted. Made her assess Noah from a fresh perspective. And she smoothed out Derrick's rough parts. Had him thinking about something other than work every second of every day.

This—what they shared—may have started off as nothing, but it was something now. At least to her. The only fear, and it was a very real fear, was that this newfound reality only ran one way.

The room spun around her. He'd pulled her up and flopped onto the mattress, taking her with him. It was not the most dignified sprawl, but she landed on top of him—exactly where she wanted to be.

She scrambled to her knees and shimmied out of her underwear then took care of getting his pants and briefs the rest of the way off. He was left wearing socks and she had the thigh-highs on. That seemed like a pretty great combination to her.

She dipped her head to kiss him and he caught her face and held her steady. Cupped her cheeks in his palms and ran a thumb over her bottom lip. "I brought the condoms home."

The practical words shot through her. It took her a second to process what he was saying, but the choice was smart and made sense. They hadn't talked the "us" part of them through yet. That first time they'd had sex had been a risk. They could get it right now.

She looked around the bedroom. "Where?"

He pointed at the nightstand next to him. "Drawer."

That was the only word he could seem to get out, which only made him sexier. As she reached, he took advantage of her unguarded position and brought his mouth to her breast. Licked all around her nipple before sucking her.

She tried to slouch on the top of his thighs, but he

held her firm. His fingers traveled down her stomach and kept going lower. Between that hot mouth and those searching fingers, she lost all sense of time and what she wanted to do next. She got lost in a swirl of energy. It thrummed through her. The tension ratcheted up as her body got nearer to the edge.

"Ellie."

She looked at his determined expression and wet lips. "Yeah?"

"Ride me."

Yes. She thought it rather than said it. Without a word, she moved over his body. Straddled those impressive hips and pressed her hands to the rippled muscles of his stomach. "Have you been a good boy?"

"Very." His finger slipped inside her.

Her muscles strained as her head fell forward. Her hair slid off her shoulders and hung down. She could feel him curl a strand around his finger.

Heat radiated off their bodies. She tore open the packet and took out the condom. It should only have taken a second to roll it over his length, but she drew it out. Squeezed him as she covered him, inch by inch. By the time she was done, he squirmed on the bed. His fingers dug into her hips as he tried to draw her closer.

Then she lifted her body up and slid over him. Every cell screamed for her to finish it, but she didn't rush this part, either. She enveloped him. Measured each second before going lower. Waited until his back lifted off the bed and his eyes glazed with need.

She could feel him pulse inside her. After all those nights of limiting themselves, their bodies craved the completion now. She ached for it. When she lifted and returned to him again, her body started to shake. She was so close.

Tiny sounds escaped her throat. She hit a steady rhythm but she couldn't hold on. Her control shattered and the orgasm tore through her, surprising her with its intensity. She could hear Derrick saying her name and feel him lift his body to meet hers. Then she couldn't think about anything except how good he felt and how much she wanted this to last.

Derrick snuck down to the kitchen about a half hour later than usual the next morning. He wanted to get Ellie a cup of coffee and serve it to her in bed. The longer he could keep her there, the happier he would be.

He hit the bottom step and knew he'd miscalculated the time. Spence was already sitting at the bar, scrolling through his cell and drinking from a mug.

He didn't lift his head as he spoke. "You're tiptoeing around your own house. That's not sad or anything."

Derrick jerked at the unexpected sound but tried to hide it. Good thing he'd put pants on or Spence would have had quite the morning show. "You're up early."

"It's about time you two slept together." Spence just kept scrolling. "All that pretending was driving me nuts. I don't know how you stood it for all those nights."

Derrick froze. "Excuse me?"

"Oh, please." Spence put his cell to the side and smiled at his brother over the top of the mug. "My door is between your bedroom and the one she goes to…and you sneak off to each night."

So much for being stealthy. Derrick should have asked her to stay in his room and forget all the subterfuge. After last night, after the hangover from the personal information he'd shared with her, he was ticked off he hadn't ended the fake part of their relationship sooner.

Screw the agreement, he wanted to actually date her. He had no idea if she could make it work, but he really wanted to try.

But that didn't mean he wanted his brother knowing all about his sex life. "That's not—"

"I could never figure out why you didn't get right into bed with her." Spence shook his head as he made a tsking sound. "She's hot. You have to be smart enough to see that."

"Careful where you go with this." The brothers didn't touch each other's dates. Not ever. That was an unspoken rule. But the real problem for Derrick was that he wasn't in top form for sparring thanks to the lack of sleep, which he did not regret one bit.

"I have eyes. I hear the way you two talk to each other." Spence's smile was far too wide and snarky for this hour. "All tinged with unspent energy."

Tinged? Yeah, way too early. "You can stop talking now."

Spence had the nerve to shrug. "I'm reporting on what I've witnessed."

"You were spying on me?" For some reason that struck Derrick as ridiculous as he leaned against the sink.

Spence hadn't asked a lot of personal questions when he'd checked in by phone over the past few months. He wasn't the type to be up in someone else's business.

"I'm trying to figure out what's happening with you." Spence drained his mug. "I promised Carter I would find out and report back."

The alarm chimed and the front door downstairs opened and closed. Only a few people knew the code and had a key. Three of them were in the house right now and one was driving cross-country to get here for what appeared to be a brotherly interrogation. That left one other option.

Jackson stepped into the room. He carried a brown bag imprinted with the name of the nearby bagel chain.

This informal breakfast looked prearranged to Derrick. Jackson didn't just stop in with snacks. His smirk didn't make his surprise appearance any less annoying.

"What's going on?" Jackson asked the room in general as he unloaded the contents of the bag onto the counter.

"I'm digging into my brother's odd relationship to figure out why it's odd," Spence said.

Jackson hesitated for a second before reaching in and pulling out a tub of cream cheese. "Aren't we all?"

"He's got it bad for her."

Derrick put his mug down and took a step toward the staircase, making sure they didn't have nosy company hovering around upstairs. "Keep your voices low."

"Are you sure it's not that you're making this complicated?" Spence shook his head. "Because, I gotta tell you. From where I'm sitting, you seem to be messing this up."

Jackson opened two drawers before he found a knife for the cream cheese. Derrick was pretty sure it was a steak knife, but it worked.

"He's not wrong about the 'messing up' part," Jackson noted.

"You like her. A lot." Jackson pointed to the bagels and kept pointing until Spence picked up a specific one. "You're kind of stupid with how much you like her."

Jackson took care of slathering the spread on one side of the bagel then handed it to Spence before giving Derrick a quick glance. "Notice he's refraining from using the bigger L-word."

"I don't want to send him running." This time Spence focused on Derrick, too. "But, really, you've got it bad for her. You're living together. So what's the holdup? Why all the weirdness?"

Derrick didn't bother answering because they really weren't talking to him. This show was for the two of them and they really seemed to be enjoying it.

Jackson shrugged. "Don't look at me. I'm waiting for an answer, too."

"Well, you both think on it while I jump in the shower." Spence shoved a large piece of bagel into his mouth and took off for the stairs.

Derrick waited until the thumping on the steps faded and Spence disappeared upstairs before saying anything. "You didn't exactly help me there."

"You need to tell him the truth." Jackson dropped the uneaten half of the bagel on the counter. "Carter is on the way. You need to tell them both. They came back to town because you asked them to. They are trying to help you, even though neither wants back in the business as your dad is insisting."

Despite the annoying display of friends-gone-wild this morning, the advice was good. Derrick knew he had to come clean. He hated lying to his brothers, anyway. But he wasn't sure what to tell them now. The thing with Ellie had started off fake. Now it felt anything but. How the hell did he describe that state?

"I will. When they're together. There's no need to tell this tale more than once." And maybe he would know the right words to say when that day came.

"And Ellie? Are you going to tell her all of it?"

"One problem at a time." Derrick leaned over and picked up the uneaten bagel half. "Until I find the right opportunity, I'll continue to fumble my way through all of this."

"I told you this would be fun to watch."

Suddenly, Derrick wasn't that hungry. "Did you?"

"Maybe I just thought it."

"I could fire you."

Jackson laughed. "But you won't."

Thirteen

Two days later Ellie was still in a good mood. She even managed to ignore the guy taking her photo as she walked into the coffee shop a few blocks from Derrick's house.

They had hit a bit of a bump at the charity event but they'd ridden through it. She wanted that to mean something. They could talk about work and their arrangement and even their families. Right from the beginning they'd vowed not to lie to each other.

Despite all that, she couldn't think of a way to broach what, a few weeks ago when they'd first met, would have been unthinkable—talking about them. She knew it was easier to ignore the elephant standing in not only the room but also right on top of them than to deal with him. "Going along as is" meant dating and living together and getting to know each other.

For her, something deeper and meaningful had grown out of that. Derrick was so much harder to read.

And he wasn't the only one. She entered the coffee shop and slipped through the long line of people waiting to order. Noah sat at a table across the room, head down and not talking to or looking at anyone. He wore a baseball cap pulled low, like every other twenty-year-old in DC, and studied his phone.

Derrick told her he'd talked with Noah but hadn't been able to break through. Seeing her brother spin and knowing he would be in very big trouble without Derrick's interference was the kind of thing that kept her up at night.

She made it the whole way to the table without him looking up. Nothing new there. Eye contact was not one of his strengths.

She pulled out a chair and sat across from him. "Why did you want to meet here?"

She'd given him her new house address. The temporary one with Derrick. Suggested he come over and they talk in private. Noah had said no to all of it.

He kept tapping buttons on his phone, only sparing a glance or two in her direction. "To avoid Derrick."

"Are you afraid of him now?" When she didn't get an immediate answer, she put a hand over the screen and lowered the phone to the table. "Well?"

"Let's say I know he'll do almost anything to get his way."

"You might want to lay off the videos because you now talk in shortcuts. It's annoying."

"Then how about this." Noah leaned forward, his elbows on the table. "He's cheating on you."

The word bounced through her. A wave of nausea followed right behind it. "What?"

"There's a woman at work."

The accusation didn't make sense. "No way."

"I'm serious, Ellie."

If Derrick had a girlfriend, then why wasn't she visiting his house? Why wasn't he using this other woman as his fake girlfriend?

How could he sleep with her but be with someone else?

Ellie couldn't imagine any woman going along with that type of ruse and all the lies. Not if she cared about Derrick and vice versa. It was too dangerous and so disrespectful. Which brought her full circle. Derrick had a lot of flaws. She could spend an hour listing them, but being crappy to women wasn't one of them. Not that she'd seen.

Too many people would have to be quiet. She'd overheard the whispers at his office and none of them were about another woman. Someone at the *Insider* would know the truth and report it.

As soon as she reasoned it out, the choking sensation in her throat eased. So did the need to pound things.

She inhaled, trying to stay focused. If she let her mind wander, she'd be on the phone or in Derrick's office demanding an explanation and she didn't want to do that. He'd been accused of enough. "You're saying you know this because you worked there?"

"I never met her. This Abby. Apparently something happened with her months ago."

That barely sounded like a thing. A bit more of her anxiety disappeared. "Noah, you're talking about rumors and not facts."

Noah spun an empty coffee cup around between his palms. The edges clicked against the table. "I'm trying to make you see that he's not worth it."

"Why?"

He closed his fist over the cup with enough force to collapse the sides with a loud crunch. "What?"

"Why is it so important to you that I think that?" That part never made sense to her. It was one thing if he thought he was falsely accused and wanted revenge. But he seemed so determined for her to think *everything* about Derrick was awful. That he wasn't only a bad boss or a mean one, but a terrible cheating human being, as well.

The whole thing struck her as overkill. Like hurt feelings and crushed emotions.

"I know what it's like to be taken in by him." Noah continued to stare at his smashed cup.

"He hired you without any experience. Gave you a job and a place to go."

Noah's head shot up. "He abandoned me as soon as he needed a scapegoat."

The conversation pinged around. Noah seemed to move from one perceived Derrick sin to another. All of them seemed to come from the same place—somewhere personal. For the first time she realized this was about way more than work or a paycheck.

She slid her hand across the table, not quite touching Noah's. "Meet with him. I'll be there and we'll talk this out."

"We've talked. He tried to convince me I was wrong when the two of us met at your apartment."

"Try again."

"Can't you just believe me?" His voice grew louder until a few people sitting nearby glanced over at them.

She refused to be derailed. "I know you're angry with him."

"Forget it." He pulled the brim of his hat down even further and stood. The legs of the chair screeched against the hard floor.

"Noah."

He finally gave her full eye contact. "I never thought you'd pick some random guy over me."

Her heart hurt. "That's not what this is."

He shrugged. "Feels like it."

Then he walked away.

Ellie was waiting for him when he got home tonight. Not upstairs in the kitchen or sitting on the couch. Not even on her laptop searching for jobs. She was actually standing at the top of the steps.

He knew that was a really bad sign.

He barely reached the second floor when she launched into her question. "Who is Abby?"

She didn't move when he got to her. No, she stood there, arms crossed, wearing what looked like a day-long-practiced frown.

He should work from home while they were in this relationship. That would stop ambushes like this from happening. "You talked with your brother."

"I tried to get through to him again."

When she didn't move, he put a hand on her arm and gently guided her into the kitchen with him. "I thought we agreed I'd handle it."

They didn't even get to the counter before she turned and faced him again. Stopped them both in their tracks. "By putting our names in the paper all the time? That's defusing his impact, but it's not stopping him for good."

The *Insider* again. The gossip column proved useful. Everyone seemed more interested in his love life than in a dispute with a former employee. No one was taking Noah seriously and he was losing viewers, which meant losing some of his power.

Derrick didn't know how people could stand to sign on and hear Noah rave about one guy all the time. That thing had to get old. It certainly had for Derrick.

So did fighting with Ellie. Usually the verbal battles invigorated him. Not the ones about Noah. Talking about him seemed to suck the life out of both of them.

He set his briefcase on the counter and brushed his fingers through her soft hair. "Any chance you could trust me?"

"I do."

It sure as hell didn't feel like it. "You're asking about Abby. You're meeting with Noah without telling me."

"And you're sounding more like my boss than…"

"What?"

"The man I'm sleeping with."

Okay, he liked that answer and since he intended to keep doing just that, he loosened his rule on talking about this subject. The Abby issue went back to his father and their family dysfunction, but there was no way to explain that without blowing his relationship with Spence apart. "Abby has nothing to do with me."

Ellie frowned at him. "Derrick, that's not an answer."

He tried again. "She works for me."

"Okay." Ellie's eyebrow lifted as if she expected more.

But to him that's exactly what Abby was—a great employee he'd fought not to lose. "That's it."

Ellie stepped away from him. She walked around the counter to sit on one of the stools. "You are making this unnecessarily difficult."

"I'm answering you."

"Did you sleep with her?" Ellie ticked off the questions on her fingers. "Are the two of you having an affair?"

"When the hell would I have time for that? I'm here with you or at work with Jackson. That's it. That's all I do."

"That answer." She shook her head. "Good grief, Derrick."

He had no idea what she wanted from him. This part of a real relationship…he wasn't a fan. People trusted him. The idea that, after a brief meeting with her brother, she no longer did, made Derrick want to rip down the walls of his house with his bare hands.

"I haven't been with anyone since I met you. I haven't even thought of anyone else since I met you." The idea of touching another woman made everything inside him rebel. "You are it for me."

The words had slipped out. He didn't mean to say them, not like that. Certainly not out loud. He was talking about her being it *for now*…right?

There were many facts stacked against them. He hadn't told her everything. They had a mess with her brother. He needed to come clean with his brothers. Hell, he wasn't even sure she liked him all that much. He could ask, but he dreaded the answer.

She was supposed to be temporary. His focus had to stay on the business and meeting his father's requirements and getting the work part of his life settled. The company meant everything to him. He'd poured so much into it. He couldn't lose focus or his father would swoop in.

That reality of his whole life being up in the air scared the hell out of him. He tried to manage everything around him and suddenly his usual skills failed him. Admitting that he might be on a road that was off his plan made him want to head to work. Do something to burn off the odd sensation running through him. This unsettled feeling he was losing control of every single part of his life.

"Right now. I mean, I feel that way right now." He had no idea why he'd added that except that he'd been trying to convince himself it was true.

Her smile fell. "Interesting qualification."

"I'm not sure what you want me to do here. I feel like there isn't a right answer." If there was, he sure as hell couldn't find it.

She sighed at him in that way that told him he was missing the mark by a mile. "Who is Abby? A real answer this time."

"She and Spence had a thing. It's complicated, and messy, and my dad screwed it all up. Honestly, it's not my story to tell. I mean, I will if you want me to, but we have a bigger issue."

"Noah." She nodded. "He delivered some envelope to the *Insider* about you cheating on me, or is about to. I think this might be your new PR issue."

"No one is going to care that a single businessman is sleeping around."

She snorted. "How comforting."

He sensed trying to explain would only make it worse, so he skipped ahead. "My point is I can fix it."

"What?"

His heart thundered in his chest. It echoed in his ears. This wasn't supposed to mean anything. They had talked about it and she had known it was coming. But taking the step proved bigger than he thought.

He forced his fingers to work. Clicking the locks, he opened the briefcase and dug around until he found the small box. The one he'd had since the day after their first date.

"This is the way we start taking control." He took the blue box out and skidded it across the marble countertop in her general direction. "Here."

She stared at it but didn't pick it up. "What are you—?"

"An engagement ring."

When she looked up at him again... That was not happiness he saw. Her teeth clenched.

"Did you hand me a box with a fake diamond ring in it?"

What the hell? "It's not fake."

"You're offended by my comment about the cost?"

The conversation was spinning away from him. He could see it, feel it. Hear the thread of anger in her voice. He ignored every warning sign and dived in. "I picked the ring out for you."

"You did?" She didn't sound even a little impressed.

"Of course. It has to look real."

She glared at him then took a turn glaring at the box. "And now you've handed it to me."

"Okay, wait a second." He rested his palms against the counter. "I don't get this. Are you upset about it being real or do you need it to be fake? Fill me in here."

She looked ten seconds away from kicking him. Derrick appreciated that there was a heavy kitchen island between them right now.

"You shoved an unopened box at me and said 'here.'" Her eyebrow lifted in challenge. "Yes?"

Okay, that sounded bad. Even he could admit that. "Uh, yeah."

"Derrick, you have to know there's a better way to do this." She waved a hand in the air. "Forget that. You should see your face. You clearly don't get it."

"Do I look confused? Because that's kind of where I am."

"Fine. I'll take this." She grabbed the box and opened it.

She made a noise that sounded like a gasp. Hesitated before picking it up. But she did pick it up. Slid it on her finger as if it didn't matter to her at all.

Yeah, this was not going well. "Wait."

"I have the ring. Next provision of our agreement satisfied. Congratulations." She slid off the bar stool and headed toward the stairs.

He didn't even realize they were done talking. "You're upset?"

"Yes, genius. I am."

"But this is what we agreed to."

She shrugged. "Then I guess we're good."

She sounded far from good. And if the kicking in his gut was any indication, he wasn't doing so great, either. "I don't understand what's happening."

"Your fake fiancée is going outside."

It was nighttime and she had a rock on her finger and a heap of attitude. "Why?"

"Because you're not there."

Ellie managed to ignore him for the rest of the night and all of the next morning. Maybe it was immature but she needed a Derrick break. He hadn't even let her walk away from him in peace. He'd texted her the second she stepped outside and said he was worried about her safety. She stayed on the front steps until she cooled off enough to go inside and walk right by him.

For the first time since she'd moved in, she missed morning coffee with him. She decided to have it with Vanessa instead. They sat in the same coffee shop where she'd had it out with her brother.

Vanessa stirred her second sugar packet into her coffee. "So, let me get this straight. He gave you a ring for a fake engagement you agreed to and now you're ticked off at him for giving it to you."

Ellie had to admit her anger sounded ridiculous when her friend put it that way. "Please don't make me sound like the unreasonable party in this."

Vanessa held up a hand in mock surrender. "I'm on your side. Always."

Silence fell over the table as Ellie tried to find the right words. She was furious and hurt. This dragging sadness exhausted her.

She hated that battered-from-the-inside gnawing sensation that overtook her when she thought about the ring and Derrick. She was not the crying type, but right now she wished she was.

She didn't even know what to say to Derrick because he wasn't wrong. She had agreed to the fake arrangement. It had just taken him longer to launch into this part than she'd expected. She'd hoped that meant something.

"It was the way he did it." And that was true. Even a fake arrangement deserved some sense of importance. He'd handed her a ring without even bothering to open the box.

Thinking about it, reliving the moment in her head, had fury bubbling up inside her again. Really, the man was clueless.

"You're angry because he didn't get on one knee and ask you?"

Ellie didn't like that question, either. "Maybe I'm not telling this story right."

"Hey, listen to me." Vanessa reached her hand across the table. "There is an obvious problem here."

"Derrick."

"Him, too. But I think the real issue is you're in love with him." Vanessa winced as she said the words.

"This is about the way he—"

Vanessa fell back in her chair. "Oh, my God. You didn't deny it."

She couldn't because she was. Vanessa said the

words and they didn't sound wrong. The realization terrified Ellie. She'd tried to be smart and careful, but she'd fallen. It was stupid and dangerous and would likely break her heart, but it happened.

She thought the truth would hit with a jolt. Instead it settled in and snuggled around her. But she still wanted to throw up.

Rather than deal with any of that, she fell back on her anger. On Derrick's depressing choices. The least he could do was fall with her.

"You don't start a fake engagement by shoving a ring at someone." How could she not see that? Ellie thought for sure she would get an immediate agreement on that topic.

Vanessa nodded. "Okay."

"Stop smiling."

"I should because I'm worried about you." The amusement left her tone. "You changed the rules in this thing. You fell for him."

"I thought… I mean, we've slept together." When Ellie realized she'd yelled that bit of information, she immediately lowered her voice. "We've gone out on these dates. None of it feels fake."

"Maybe that's what the two of you need to talk—" Vanessa stopped herself midsentence then leaned in closer. "You're not confronting this because you're afraid the relationship didn't change for him."

Exactly. That was it. She should clear all this up. But what if the answer was something other than what she wanted it to be? "Maybe I should sell the ring and move to Alaska."

Vanessa's eyes bulged. "Wait, is that thing real?"

"He said it was." Ellie studied it for the fiftieth time. It was stunning. Big. But not too much. A solitaire surrounded by smaller diamonds, and a perfect fit. She didn't even want to know how he'd pulled that off.

"Damn. Go Derrick."

Anger or not, the ring made a statement. "Right?"

"I'm going to give you some advice."

Ellie didn't hide her groan. "About shoes? That's about all I can handle right now."

"You need to end this."

Her stomach went into free fall. "Did you miss the *in love with him* part?"

"That's my point. You guys need a do-over. Start fresh and honest."

"We've been honest with each other." With a few false starts, they had made a deal. They'd both known, going in, what this was and what it would mean: solving problems for both of them and little more.

Well, damn. Vanessa was right. She was the one who changed the deal.

"Since you're here and not with him, I think that's not true." Ellie started to talk and Vanessa talked over her. "You did storm out, right?"

"I do not storm."

She rolled her eyes. "I've seen you storm."

"He makes me want to throw things."

"Not the ring." Vanessa picked up Ellie's hand and gave the ring a closer inspection. "You're keeping that if the knucklehead doesn't get his act together. I mean, come on."

"The problem is I want to keep it all—his friends,

his house, his brother." The words ripped out of Ellie. It hurt to admit all of that.

"Oh, man. You have it bad."

Ellie was starting to realize that. "No kidding."

Fourteen

"He didn't actually steal the money." Derrick said the comment more to himself than to any one person. He'd forgotten Jackson was sitting in the chair across from him, one leg crossed over the other, so he did have a captive audience.

He looked up. "Excuse me?"

Derrick wasn't sure how to explain how he'd come to that conclusion, but he tried, anyway. It was more of a feeling than any one specific grounded in fact. Still, he thought he'd stumbled over the right answer. "It was this thing Noah said. He talked about being my mentee."

From the beginning Derrick had assumed the situation with Noah was about money. That fact fit with what he knew about Ellie's precarious finances and now with what he knew about her unstable upbringing and the limited resources and attention given to Noah.

Noah hadn't been searching for easy money. He hadn't even tried to take the amount he'd managed to gather out of the account he'd created, which would have been easy. He'd moved the money the same way he'd moved around everything else in the company's system. Without one person noticing. And Derrick hired smart people. They knew what they were doing but their brains were no match for Noah's. He'd acted almost as if he were bored and looking for a better way to categorize things.

Derrick's tech people were still trying to figure out how the kid's mind worked so they could mimic it.

"You know you've been sitting for three hours without moving."

"So?"

"You worked late last night." Jackson nodded in the direction of Derrick's cell. "You haven't been texting with Ellie today like you usually do."

Derrick had no idea what that had to do with the information Jackson mentioned, except to question why he spent so much time tracking Derrick's movements. "I'm working."

"Are you sure you're not pouting?" Jackson dropped the file he was looking at on his lap. Closed the cover and focused on Derrick instead.

"Does that seem like something I'd do?"

Jackson snorted. "Not before Ellie."

Derrick didn't know how he felt about that answer,

either. He knew she'd turned his life upside down. He'd lost control of his office and his home but he'd hoped no one else had picked up on that.

While they were spinning around topics without finding answers, he figured he might as well add one more fact. "We're engaged, by the way."

Jackson's foot fell to the floor. "What?"

Derrick returned to looking at the printouts in front of him. "I need you to send out that press release and leak the info to the *Insider*."

That was the game, after all. A fake engagement to clean up his reputation and defuse Noah. The idea had once made sense but Derrick had grown to hate the words. Now he wanted a shot at making it real.

"Back up." Jackson knocked his fist against the desktop. "When did this big event happen?"

"Yesterday." A day that now ranked as one of the most confusing days of Derrick's life.

He'd thought he was doing the right thing when he'd taken out the box. Settling the unsettled between them. Giving Noah another reason to calm down. Feeding the PR machine. But he'd forgotten that Ellie didn't always do and say what he expected. She worked in this other world that he didn't get.

Bottom line, he'd hurt her and she didn't seem ready to let him fix the damage. That might have been good since he had no idea *how* to fix it.

"And we aren't celebrating the big event?" Jackson asked.

There would be a party. That was the point. A public coming-out of sorts. But he had one problem with arranging it right now… "She hasn't talked to me since."

Jackson laughed. "That sounds like a good start to a marriage."

"A fake marriage." For some reason everyone kept forgetting that part. Sure, the ring was real. It seemed like a dick move to get her a fake one of those. Besides, he liked the idea of her wearing his ring. Of seeing it on her finger.

He was totally losing it. He no longer knew exactly what he wanted. His emotions bounced back and forth along with his priorities.

Jackson exhaled long and loud. "We're back to that. The damn agreement you two signed."

"Did we ever leave it?"

Jackson tapped his pen against his folder. The clicking sound thumped through the room. "Derrick, what did you do?"

Derrick wanted to dig in to his work. Buying properties, selling properties, building properties. He could assess a piece of land and pinpoint its future value, see what it could be once he was done with it.

Figuring out Ellie? He needed a team of experts for that mission. Maybe Jackson could be on it. "What do you mean?"

Jackson exhaled a second time. "How did you ask her?"

"You're coming up with a lot of questions." For some reason that made Derrick nervous. Very little made him nervous.

"Maybe answer one."

"I gave her the ring." There. Simple.

Jackson's pen stopped midtap. "Gave?"

Since Ellie had treated him to a similar response, Derrick decided to stall. His delivery of the ring had been off. He got that now. Interesting how everyone seemed to know the fake engagement rules better than he did.

"Can you only talk in questions now?" he asked, ignoring the irony of that.

"What do you think?"

Some days it was hard to like Jackson. "Very funny."

"When you say 'gave,' you mean you asked her…" Jackson made a face. "Please mean that."

"No."

"Ah, I see." Jackson coughed, clearly trying to hide a smile. "How did that romantic gesture go over?"

"I slept alone last night, so not well." Derrick had walked to her door. Before they'd started sleeping together, every night he'd knock and go in. Once they were together and not fighting the sex, where she slept hadn't been a question…until yesterday.

"Do you really not see the problem or what your contribution to the mess you're in now actually was?" Jackson asked.

Of course he did. *Now.* "No."

"Damn it. I'm going to lose that bet."

That stopped Derrick. "What bet?"

"The one I made with Spence."

"Want to fill me in?"

"You'll figure it out." Jackson stood and took out his cell. "If you don't, I'm out two hundred dollars, so please figure it out fast."

"I'm here as ordered." Noah sat at Derrick's dining room table. "I'm not sure why we couldn't meet at the coffee place again."

"Because I can't go outside without having my picture taken." Ellie had about reached the end of her patience on that subject. She glanced to where Derrick sat at the head of the table. "We're going to talk about that, by the way."

His gaze went to her ring then bounced to her face. "What did you expect would happen?"

He had an uncanny knack for saying the wrong thing at the wrong time. The man built an impressive enterprise that churned out money, yet he failed on a simple people skills level some days. She might lecture him about that, too.

Noah frowned at both of them. "What's happening? Why am I here?"

"We're clearing the air."

Noah started to get up as soon as Derrick stopped speaking. "No, thanks."

"Sit." Derrick issued the order. "We're also engaged."

He really would be the death of her. Ignoring Noah's stunned expression, she glared at Derrick. "Really? That's how you drop that information?"

"If you have a script you want me to follow, please let me know."

He was in fine Derrick form today. He shot back the one-liners faster than she could come up with them on her end.

Noah sat hard in the chair again. The thud seemed to wake him out of his stupor. "What are you talking about? You can't marry him."

Through the haze of frustration winding around her, she could see him. She and Derrick might have an odd arrangement they worked out, but that didn't mean her brother was prepared for the roller coaster they'd all jumped on.

"Noah, let me explain." Though she had no idea what she could say.

"At least wait until you see this video." Noah slipped a thumb drive out of his jeans' pocket and dumped it on the table.

"What's on it?" Derrick asked.

Noah didn't even spare him a glance. "I bet you'd like to know."

"I can take it and watch it right now or you can save us some time and talk." Derrick snatched the drive and held it in the air.

"You and your father and a certain woman at work."

"This is old news." Derrick shook his head. "This is about Abby, right? I'm not sure where you're getting your information but Abby dated my brother. Not me."

Noah blinked a few times. "That's not what Joe—"

Ellie wasn't about to let Noah stop there. "Who?"

Noah shook his head. "Nothing."

"Joe Cantor? Is he the one who's been feeding you false intel, hoping you'd fall for it?" Derrick asked.

"Joe?" Ellie thought her head might explode.

The ramifications of what Noah admitted flowed through her brain. Joe had planted that story in the *Insider* about her work. He was trying to undermine Derrick and his relationship with Spence. And this poor Abby person was stuck in the middle. Sure, Derrick had made Joe look stupid, but the timing didn't seem right. And what kind of man would take that bait and go to all this trouble?

"You've been working with my former boss?" It sounded awful when she said it out loud. "The one who kicked me out of the office and sent me home without a paycheck?"

"It's not like that." Noah shook his head. "Only in the last few weeks when you guys started dating."

"Let's run through this." Derrick's firm voice broke through the room. "The *Insider* is not running anything about me cheating, because I'm not and they don't want to be sued."

"How did you—"

"And…" Derrick talked right over Noah's explanation or whatever else he was going to say. "If you put up that video, you'll hurt Abby. Not me. She deserves better than that. Honestly, she's been screwed over by my family enough without adding yours."

Noah shook his head. "Don't try—"

"Why did you move the money? Was Joe involved in that?"

Derrick's question came out of nowhere. Ellie had no idea what he was talking about.

But Noah didn't look even a little confused. "It's about time you figured it out, but Joe's not involved."

Ellie rushed to keep up. "What are you two talking about?"

"Noah moved money out of a bunch of work accounts and moved it into a fake client account he designed. Hid it all but didn't actually take it. I just figured that out." Derrick's gaze switched from her to Noah again. "So, did you run out of time to make a withdrawal?"

"I was never going to take it. I just wanted to prove I could do it."

It was such a Noah thing to say that Ellie's heart melted. He refused to see the results of his choices. He acted and let everyone else clean up his mess. Whatever his issues, he had to learn a new way. "Oh, Noah."

"You brought me on at the office then put me in that room." Noah ignored her and turned on Derrick. "I tried to talk with you about problems in your system, but you said I had to talk with my direct boss."

Derrick's eyes narrowed. "You were trying to get my attention."

"Don't flatter yourself." Noah returned to staring at the table.

That was it. Ellie knew Derrick was right. Something in Noah's reaction or Derrick's tone. In the middle of their fight and Noah's threats, Derrick had gotten to the bottom of the stealing question. He wasn't blaming. He was laying out facts. Because he was a good man. A man worth loving. The man she'd fallen for.

This time the realization didn't make her want to throw up. She wanted to tear up that ridiculous agreement so she'd never have to think about it again.

Derrick shifted in his chair, clearly trying to get Noah to look at him again. "I didn't mean to ignore you in the office."

Noah snorted. "Stop acting like I cared."

But he did. No matter what Noah was saying, he did. It all made sense now. So many people ignored Noah and passed him over. They didn't take the time to see what he could do. Derrick had taken an interest in him. Hired him without a load of experience or an advanced degree.

Derrick had taken a chance and Noah had taken that to mean something more than the usual employer/employee relationship. Derrick never could have seen this coming.

"I asked the prosecutor not to move ahead with the charges," Derrick said in a low voice.

The sound shot through her. The words…he'd kept his promise. Of course he did.

Derrick looked at her then. "For you and for him."

"You're not doing me any favors." But all of the anger had left Noah's voice. His outburst died as soon as the words were out. "Ellie, listen to me. You can't marry him."

"It's happening," Derrick said.

Noah stood. "I'll be back when he's not here."

That comment struck her as silly. "It's his house."

"Leave the video," Derrick said.

"Because you say so?"

Derrick shook his head. "Because I'm asking you not to release it."

"Fine." Noah slammed the drive onto the table and walked out.

Derrick watched Noah go. Apparently storming out in a huff was a Gold family tradition. Ellie did it better, but Noah was pretty good at it. Even slammed the front door.

Ellie stood. Derrick half expected her to go upstairs and not talk again this evening like a repeat of last night. He fought to find the right words to say but nothing came to him.

She stopped next to his chair. Her hand slipped into

his. When she gave his arm a gentle tug, he figured she wanted him to stand.

The change in her mood confused him. "Are you okay?"

Instead of answering him, she kissed him. Her arms slipped around his neck and she pulled his head to her. Then her mouth met his and speaking wasn't on his mind.

Her tongue licked out to caress his bottom lip. She had his brain misfiring and his pants growing tighter. It took all the strength he possessed to lift his head and stare at her, to drag his mouth away from hers. "You don't need to thank me this way."

He waited for her shoulders to stiffen, for her anger to rise.

She pressed a finger to his lips. Traced the outline before letting her finger trail down his throat to his chest. "You told me once that I should only kiss you if I wanted to kiss you."

The sound of her deep voice was enough to touch off something inside him. He got hard and his resistance to her, what little he still had, melted. "That's still the rule."

"I want to kiss you."

It took a second for her words to register in his brain. She wanted him. Through the missteps and the battles, after sleeping alone, she still wanted him.

Still, they'd been through some hard days. "Be sure."

She pressed her hand against his chest, backing him up until his butt hit the wall. "I am. I choose you, Derrick. Not because of an arrangement or money or my brother. I want you because of you."

That's all it took. The last of his defenses fell. Every argument for why he should hold back and not let this mean anything vanished.

His body vetoed his brain. They could talk later. They needed this now.

His mouth met hers in a kiss meant to possess. He wanted her to know this was real. There was nothing fake about how much he wanted to touch her, to be inside her. His hands traveled over her as she unbuttoned his shirt. She reached the bottom few and tugged. Buttons ripped off and pinged against the floor.

It was a wild frenzy to disrobe. He wanted her naked but settled for shoving her skirt up to her waist and tugging her bikini underwear down. Their legs tangled and he leaned against the wall for balance. When that didn't get him what he wanted, he spun them around.

With her spine pressed against the wall, he lifted her legs to his hips and settled his body between them. Her ankles balanced against his ass as he held her with one hand and rushed to unzip with the other.

Chaos filled his mind. A wild energy pounded through him. All he could think about was being inside her, of feeling her body wrap around his. At the last second, he slowed. His finger went to the very center of her. When he found her wet and ready, he slipped into fast forward again.

"I'm going to help your brother, Ellie," Derrick said between stinging kisses.

She put her palms against his cheeks and forced him to look at her. "Yes, but later."

"Much later."

Then he was inside her. He plunged in and stopped.

Ignored the sexy little growling sounds she made and just enjoyed the tight grip of her body around his.

She pinched his shoulder. "Derrick, move."

This one time he was happy to obey.

Fifteen

The DC Insider: *The party is on! We admit
we were worried Derrick Jameson blew it,
but friends and family are gathering. There's
word of a sparkly dress and champagne being
brought in by the truckload. Let the marriage
plans begin.*

Two more weeks of tentative peace passed. Ellie returned to Derrick's bedroom. He hadn't proposed in
a better way, but he did spend some time each night
touching her ring. His finger smoothed over it with a
near reverence. He'd spin it around on her finger as
he watched in awe.

She still didn't understand him. His mood stayed
relatively steady but he worked too much and continued to say the odd stray comment that made her

wonder how often he dealt with actual human beings other than her.

A month had passed since they'd first slept together. After a detour to help a friend, Carter was on the way, which meant she would know both brothers soon. Even Derrick's father was flying in with his relatively new wife.

The idea of that made Ellie's stomach flip over. That was a lot of Jamesons in one house. She hoped they didn't kill each other. Even she thought about punching Derrick's father. The man had made a big mess of his family then snuck away to let Derrick clean it all up. What kind of man was that?

Friends and relatives officially would start pouring into town in two days. The party, the sheer scope of it, made no sense to Ellie. A hundred people. She didn't know five people she'd want in her house. This family had business associates and relatives everywhere.

This was the kind of shindig you threw when you really planned to walk down the aisle. Family met family. Friends traded stories. The happy couple showed off photos of their time together so far. None of that fit their situation, yet Derrick insisted.

He still hadn't filled Spence in about the truth of their relationship. Ellie hadn't because she no longer saw any part of what they shared as fake.

Jackson and Derrick had been trapped in the library all morning. There was talk of moving the party to the Jameson's Virginia property and holding it outside under the most expensive tent she had ever seen in her life. The thing had actual doors and windows.

She'd never seen the farm in person, but from the photos she thought it looked like a school. The idea that Derrick grew up there without his mom and with a distant father made her ache for him. The loneliness had to have been unbearable. Her parents had made a lot of mistakes, but they'd been around. Broke and confusing, but present.

She grabbed a mug of tea and headed for the library to see what ridiculous plans the men had dreamed up while she'd dressed this morning. She'd been dragging all week. She'd only ever needed about six hours of sleep each night. She'd swear she could use twice that much right now.

The stress was working on her. There was no other explanation. It also messed with her stomach. Coffee made it grumble these days.

If she were honest, she'd have to admit she didn't feel great. A terrible cold might be headed her way. When she'd mentioned that to Derrick last night he'd made her promise it would come after the party. As if she could control life like that.

She sipped on the herbal mixture of lemon and peppermint. The warm liquid poured through her on the chilly spring day. She'd thrown on one of Derrick's sweaters and it swamped her. She didn't care. The soft material made her think of a blanket.

The closer she got to the room, she expected the voices to grow louder. They didn't. The door was open an inch or two. She pushed it open a smidgen. Took the opportunity to watch them.

Even at home, Derrick stayed in command. He wore black pants and a simple white shirt. On him, the combination proved stunning. She was about to tell him that, maybe embarrass him a little in front of

Jackson, which was always fun, when she heard the ominous sentence.

You have to stop lying to Ellie.

She pushed the door open the whole way. Immediately she was greeted by the stares of the two men and Jackson's mouth dropped open. Derrick didn't show any reaction at all but his watchful eyes followed her.

"Lying about what?" That was the only question that ran through her head so she asked it.

Lies. The word stuck in her throat. She turned it over and tried to make it fit with everything she knew about Derrick and the upcoming party. Nothing matched the urgency she'd heard in Jackson's tone.

She couldn't ignore the comment. She'd grown up with lies. She'd lived with so many over the years and knew how they could burn away all the other good things in life. They stole security. She'd lost her job over one.

But Derrick had promised not to lie to her. He'd said it more than once. It was one of the underlying principles of their agreement.

Time ticked by and neither man answered her.

She stepped closer. For a second the room began to spin. The walls of books blurred and she would have stumbled but she fought for balance.

"Someone answer me," she said in a louder voice. She would yell if she had to.

Jackson looked at Derrick. "I should go."

"Don't move." She wasn't letting either of them off the hook because this was clearly big. "Someone start talking."

"There was another reason for our agreement."

Derrick's deep voice broke through the otherwise quiet room.

"The fake engagement." The words scraped against her throat.

"What started out as that, yes."

She ignored the comment. Pretended his words didn't echo what she'd wanted for the past few weeks—a real chance with him.

Her head started to pound. The drumming sensation started at the base of her neck. After a few more steps, it moved up to her nape. Her footsteps faltered. At first she thought her shoe had snagged the carpet, but no. Her balance was off. The room tilted on her.

"Explain." She somehow got the word out.

"My father said he would sell the business out from under me unless I met certain stipulations."

Eldrick Jameson. She should have known he was at the bottom of this. That bit of information fit everything Derrick had ever told her about his father. The man was pure trouble. He caused trouble, incited it.

But none of that explained Jackson's comment.

"What does that have to do with me?" She could no longer stand there. She set the mug down, ignoring her shaking hand.

"Are you okay?" Jackson asked, the concern obvious in his voice.

"Finish it, Derrick." Because she knew there was more. This all related to her. All that talk at the beginning of their relationship about how they were helping each other. Yes, she'd let herself get sucked in because he'd wanted to. But the reasoning rang hollow now.

"Each brother has an obligation they have to meet or we lose everything. My obligation was multipart.

I had to lure my brothers back to the business and I had to clean up my image."

That didn't sound so bad. It was close to what she knew with a few holes filled in. "Okay."

"I told you I needed your brother to stop. I didn't tell you my continued ownership of the business depended on it. Depended on you."

"The deal was pretty lopsided," Jackson said.

"I needed you more than you needed me. Without you, I lost everything." Derrick hesitated for a few seconds. "For me this wasn't about helping Noah. It was about keeping control of the business."

"That's pretty ruthless." The room started to blur along the edge. She looked at him through this strange haze.

She had no idea what was happening. It was as if her body was shutting down, abandoning her. But she refused to give in. She wanted all of this information out between them. No more secrets.

"I never pretended to be anything but ruthless," Derrick said.

That wasn't true. She'd thought so at first, but that was part of his perfectly crafted image. The real man was much more complex. Decent.

"Why not tell me the truth?" That part didn't make sense to her.

Derrick never left his place by the fireplace. He held on to the mantel as if it were the one thing holding him up. "I didn't know you and didn't want you to have the upper hand against me."

"Weeks ago. But now?" She shook her head and almost dropped to her knees.

Jackson got up from his chair and Derrick took

a step forward. She waved them both back. "Why, Derrick?"

"I didn't want what we had to stop."

The sex. He liked the sex and was willing to tell her half-truths and use her to keep getting it. "Maybe you are ruthless."

She saw Derrick rush forward and heard Jackson yell. Everything moved in slow motion as the air whooshed around her. Before she could call out, the pain closed over her and the room went dark.

Pregnant. Not just pregnant but a high-risk pregnancy.

Derrick sat beside Ellie's hospital bed and turned the doctor's words over in his head. He'd been pummeled with information since they'd arrived in the emergency room. Now she was settled in a private room and the facts still didn't make sense.

Spence and Jackson had stood next to him, taking it all in. Derrick had barely heard a thing. All he could think about was the ambulance ride. The first responders yelling, talking to the hospital. The noise as they'd driven at high speed. The beep of the machine next to him.

It had been a flurry of activity. Everyone rushed and ran. The stretcher. The blood from where her head had hit the floor before he could catch her. He'd thrown up twice while he'd waited for the doctor to come out and deliver some news.

And the news…pregnancy.

Now he had to tell her because this was not the ideal situation. Forget the state of their engagement. He would fix that as soon as she let him. He knew what he wanted now. Watching her fall, thinking he'd lost her, shifted his whole world into focus.

He'd told her he'd kept part of the truth about the agreement from her because he hadn't wanted their time together to end. What he hadn't said was that he loved her. He was couldn't-think-straight in love with her.

That losing her made him double over.

That he would forfeit the business if it meant she would stay with him.

His thumb slipped over the engagement ring on her finger and he thought back to the silly way he'd given it to her. So dismissive, ignoring her feelings. Jackson had unloaded, letting him know every way he'd messed up.

Derrick knew it was Jackson's way of handling his fear. Derrick's was to bury his brain in work and he couldn't do that now.

"Derrick?"

At the sound of her rough voice, he looked at her. Her eyes were open and filled with fear.

"Hey." He brushed her hair off her cheek. "You're okay."

"What happened?"

The worst. His nightmare. "You fainted."

But he'd thought it was something else. He'd never dreamed the answer would be pregnancy. He could handle that, or he would learn how to. But watching her drop...he never wanted to see that again.

"I did?" She tried to sit up.

He gently pushed her down. She'd be in the hospital for a few days. They had decisions to make. There were tests to run and precautions to take.

"My head is killing me." She lifted a hand and the tubes attached to her arm went with her.

"You're on an IV." He glanced at the bag hanging on the hook by his head. "You have some meds."

"What's wrong?"

He took a deep breath. "Well, here's some news. You can get pregnant with an IUD."

Her eyes widened. "What?"

"It's rare but it happens." He slipped his fingers through hers. "You're about five weeks along."

What little color was in her face drained away. Then her hand went to her stomach in a protective gesture that tugged at his heart.

"The first time we slept together," she said.

"Yeah." He didn't want her to be in danger but it was hard to want to call that night back. It had started them down this road.

She swallowed a few times before talking again. "Tell me all of it."

She deserved to know, so he didn't hide behind calls for her to wait or for rest.

"It means this is a risky pregnancy. Taking the IUD out now can be a problem. Leaving it in can, too." He swallowed before saying the part that made his voice break. "There's an increased chance of miscarrying and a lot of precautions we'll need to take if you decide you want to go through with the pregnancy."

Tears filled her eyes. "I understand."

So brave. No surprise there.

He leaned over and placed a sweet kiss on her forehead. "I will support whatever you want to do."

"You don't have to… I told you about the birth control, but…" This time the tears rolled down her cheeks.

"We created this baby together. Both of us."

She nodded but didn't say anything.

The quiet tears tore at him. "I will be with you no matter what."

She closed her eyes and nodded. The tears still fell harder. "I need to sleep."

"Okay." He had no idea if that was normal for her condition or if she was shutting off. He didn't want to ask. "I'll be right here."

"You do love her."

Derrick looked up an hour later to find Noah and Spence standing in the hospital room doorway.

"He wanted to see his sister," Spence said.

"Of course."

Derrick was more grateful for Jackson and Spence than ever. They stayed calm while he nearly lost it. He'd cradled Ellie, making sure she was breathing. They'd made the calls.

Noah came into the room then. He walked over to Ellie's bedside and stared at her. "She's really pregnant?"

Derrick couldn't believe it, either. "Yes, but it's risky."

Noah nodded without looking up. "Spence told me."

Spence. Interesting. Derrick hoped that meant they'd bonded. Noah needed guidance.

"Thanks."

The word came out soft. Derrick almost missed it.

"I'm not going to let anything happen to her, Noah." Derrick thought about what Noah had said about a mentee. "If you let me, I'll make it up to both of you."

"I shouldn't have moved the money."

"No."

"We can worry about that later," Spence said.

Noah nodded again as he stepped away from the bed. "I want to get her some flowers."

"I know the place for that." Spence gestured for Noah to follow then winked at Derrick.

He watched them go and thought about all that had happened. All the miscommunication and missed cues. He'd hidden behind his desk for so long, so focused on the business and not the people he cared about. But no more. He would do better. For her, he would try.

Sixteen

The DC Insider: *An ambulance. A family fight. These Jamesons know how to keep things interesting. But the fairy tale is back on! Congratulations to Derrick Jameson and Ellie Gold on their upcoming wedding...and the little surprise they've been keeping. We're hoping for a girl.*

Ellie was finally able to leave the hospital three days later. Not that anyone let her even take a step on her own. She'd tried to get off the couch for a drink of water this morning and men had come from every direction.

Derrick had turned away the engagement party guests. He'd explained that Ellie was sick. She didn't know much else because every time she opened her mouth Derrick tried to feed her or give her a pill.

The guy loved playing nurse. She let it happen because she worried about what would happen when he stopped. The game should be over. Everyone knew everything now. Noah had been by every day. He seemed connected to Spence's side and had made a tentative peace with Derrick.

She must have *really* been sick.

She heard male voices and Derrick's telling people to get out. His tone, frustrated and gruffer than usual, made her tense. She'd been waiting for bad news since she got home. Not that she needed to invite more.

Derrick hadn't been overstating what they faced with this pregnancy. It carried all sorts of risks. Not as bad as it could have been because she hadn't been that far along when they'd discovered it, but the risks were still pretty high. So she'd opted for keeping the IUD. Now she spent every day doubting the choice and worrying she'd lose the baby. Derrick's baby.

After everything that happened, she still wanted to build something with him. But could she trust him? He'd kept most of his promises to her, but he still lied. At the very least, he held information back because it benefitted him. She couldn't figure out a way to process that.

"Hey." That's all Derrick said as he walked into the room.

Just as he had since she'd come home, he seemed subdued and a bit on edge. Her insides churned and she half wondered if that rubbed off on him.

She tapped the couch cushion next to her. "Can you come sit with me for a second?"

He hesitated then nodded. "Everything okay?"

He'd asked her that so many times that she now dreaded the question. "Is it, Derrick?"

"What does that mean?"

The question had been right there, on her tongue. She'd bit it back for days. Didn't want to invite trouble. But she had to know. "Do you want me to leave?"

He made an odd face. "What?"

"This relationship was fake and now that—"

He swore under his breath. The sound of the harsh words made her jump. She wasn't afraid but he did let them fly. She started to get up, but he held her hands and pulled her closer to his side.

"Never."

The word didn't make any sense. "What?"

His chest visibly rose as he inhaled a deep breath. "Ellie, how can you not get this? I love you."

She didn't realize she was shaking her head until he touched her hair. "What?"

"I fell in love with you. Nothing about this or how I feel about you is fake."

Her mind refused to believe and that made his words that much sharper. "You don't mean that."

This was about guilt and the baby. He'd been moping around, not going to work. The pressure…she got it. It crushed her, too.

"We can figure something…" She didn't even know what to say. She'd practiced and now the words wouldn't come.

He slid off the couch and went to one knee. "Ellie Gold."

She froze. "What's happening?"

"Go ahead." Spence called out the encouragement from the top of the stairs. Jackson stood with him and Vanessa. Noah was there. And was Spence holding up a phone?

Jackson pointed at the cell's screen. "Carter didn't want to miss this. He's still ticked off that Derrick didn't tell the whole truth, either."

"You mention that now?" Derrick swore again. "You're all pains in the—"

"Keep going," Vanessa called out.

"Fine." But Derrick didn't sound fine. His voice was sharp and he was fidgeting. Something he rarely did. Then he looked at her and the scowl disappeared. A softness moved into his eyes. "Hi."

"Hi." She had no idea what else to say.

"I think I loved you from the first time I met you." He laughed then. "You were so unimpressed with me and who I was. So beautiful and not interested in anything I had to say. It was a potent combination."

The room started spinning again. This didn't have anything to do with her pregnancy or fainting. It was the punch of happiness—hope—that seared through her. It left her breathless.

"I should have told you everything from the start, but I didn't want you to find a new place to live." Derrick laughed as he bent to kiss her hand. "Hell, it took forever to get you to agree to share a bed with me."

He reached out a hand and fit it over her stomach. "Not that long, I guess."

"Derrick…" She didn't know what she wanted to say except his name.

"What I should have said when I gave you this ring." He held it up.

They'd taken it off her in the hospital and she hadn't dared ask for it. She felt naked and half-sick without it. Relief nearly swamped her at seeing it again.

He turned it over in his fingers. "I picked this because it reminded me of you. Bold, sparkly, beautiful. Different in every perfect way."

Her defenses, already shaky, collapsed. Seeing him kneeling there, usually so strong but now so vulnerable, won her over. He'd messed up but they could fix this. They could learn to communicate better, to share. Together, they'd unlearn some of the damaging interpersonal skills passed down from their parents. They would do better.

She reached out and cupped his cheek. "Yes."

He shook his head but this time he was smiling. "No, I'm asking this time."

She bit back a laugh because he seemed so determined.

"Ellie Gold, I love you more than anything. I loved you before I knew about the pregnancy and I'll love you forever, if you let me."

"Yes." The word rushed out of her. She was laughing and crying and nodding. One big weepy mess.

"Marry me."

This time she fell against his chest and felt his strong arms wrap around her. He whispered something into her hair. She could hear her name and the cheers from their family and friends who were sharing the moment. She loved all of it, all of them; mostly she loved Derrick.

She pulled back and stared up at him. Derrick, the strong and determined man who liked to boss her around and argue for no good reason. With him she felt the intoxicating mix of comfort and heat. She loved him and wanted him. She knew he would help protect their baby and they'd save each other if they lost it.

"I love you." Her voice was soft but mighty.

"About time you said that." He rested his forehead against hers. "I'm going to need to hear it a lot."

"You know, if this is a real engagement—"

"It is." He practically barked the response at her.

"You should know that I plan to be a bossy fiancée and an even bossier wife." And that was an understatement.

Once she checked with the doctor about what she could do and couldn't, she'd try to return to the work she loved. She'd also control his schedule a bit better than he did. No more all-nighters in the office or dinners at ten. She was going to get his life in line.

"Wait, what?" But he didn't sound even a little worried about the idea.

"We'll start with your work hours." She glanced over his head at Jackson. "They are decreasing."

He nodded. "Yes, ma'am."

Derrick cleared his throat. "We'll talk."

"I'll win." She looked around and realized she already had.

"I can hardly wait to negotiate our new agreement."

She heard groans that matched the one she was holding back. "You're not going to believe what provisions I add."

He kissed her then. Long and lingering. When he lifted his head, all the stress he'd carried on his face for the past few days was gone. "You can have everything you want."

Her heart swelled. "You're going to be a great husband."

Carter would arrive tomorrow, after what had turned out to be a ten-day trip across the country. Only his baby brother would draw out something like that.

"What are you laughing about?" Spence asked.

Derrick looked up to see Spence staring at him. He stood at the kitchen sink, nursing his morning coffee. Ellie wasn't up yet, which Derrick assumed would become a new thing now that she was pregnant.

They had a wedding and a baby ahead of them. His father was coming for the rescheduled engagement party in a few weeks. All of the things Derrick never thought he'd have, a family of his own and the stability of friends and family around him, were happening.

"Life is pretty good," he said in response to his brother's question.

"For you." Spence shook his head. "You've met Dad's conditions. Noah is quiet, your PR image is pristine, and Carter and I are both here, at least for the short-term. For as long as you need us, actually."

"Thanks."

"Yeah, well. Apparently, I'm up next. Dad has some stipulations Carter and I need before we can settle the business and get him out for good."

"You don't have to—"

Spence made a strange noise. "I do."

Derrick didn't want to subject his brothers to their father's stipulations, to have them run around trying to meet his conditions. He was willing to stop the nonsense. The business used to mean everything but his priorities had shifted. He knew he'd survive without the office now.

"This isn't up for debate, Derrick." Spence stared at him. "Got it? No more secrets or arguing."

That loyalty meant more to Derrick than he ever thought possible. "Yes."

"And the business is yours." Spence smiled over

his mug. "Just do a good job once Dad steps fully out so I can keep collecting the checks for my minority interest."

Derrick lifted his mug in a fake toast. "Happy to."

"And we'll be here for you and for Ellie." He made a groaning sound. "Even for Noah."

Noah was one more thing Derrick needed to deal with. But not today. For the next week, Ellie was his only priority. He was stepping aside and letting Jackson do what Jackson did best—run things.

He had a party to plan and a wedding to set. There were about a billion doctor's appointments they needed to go to. A bunch of specialists. He vowed that Ellie would not go through any of it alone.

"I appreciate that." Derrick let his mind wander to the one place he didn't want to go. "With this pregnancy—"

"She needs you. We'll take up the slack and do Dad's bidding."

Derrick had no idea how to thank Spence for that. He tried anyway. "I truly appreciate that."

Spence put down the mug and moved to the other side of the kitchen island, across from Derrick. "Stop doing that."

"What?"

"Being grateful." He snorted. "It's annoying."

"Only you would think so."

"We're going to get through this. She's going to be fine—so is the baby."

Derrick needed to hear the words. They might be empty, but he could tell Spence believed them. That was enough for now. "I believe I remember something about a bet?"

"Hell, no. You weren't in on it."

Derrick held out his hand. "Two hundred or I tell Ellie."

"Unbelievable." Spence slipped his wallet out of his pocket. "You only get this if I have a chance to win it back."

That sounded ominous but Derrick took the cash anyway. "How?"

"Give me the baby's due date so I have the inside scoop and can take a bunch of Carter's money."

"Sold." The sound of their laughter filled the kitchen.

For the first time ever, Derrick finally felt like he was home.

* * * * *

Look for Spence's story,
coming in summer 2018!

COMING NEXT MONTH FROM

◆ HARLEQUIN®
Desire

Available February 6, 2018

#2569 FOR THE SAKE OF HIS HEIR
Billionaires and Babies • by Joanne Rock

A marriage of convenience is decidedly inconvenient for Brianne Hanson when the groom is her sexy boss! Resisting Gabe was already tough, but now that they're sharing a bed, it's only a matter of time before she gives in to his seductions...

#2570 RICH RANCHER'S REDEMPTION
Texas Cattleman's Club: The Impostor • by Maureen Child

Jesse Navarro knows he doesn't deserve the gorgeous Jillian Norris, but he can't seem to stay away. After one amazing, mistaken red-hot night, will his dark past stand in the way of love?

#2571 THE BABY CLAIM
Alaskan Oil Barons • by Catherine Mann

Billionaire Broderick Steele was raised to hate his rival, Glenna Mikkelson-Powers. Even if she's the sexiest woman he's ever known. Then, amid corporate mergers and scandal, they find an abandoned baby who could be Broderick's...or Glenna's. Playing house has never been so high-stakes!

#2572 RAGS TO RICHES BABY
Millionaires of Manhattan • by Andrea Laurence

When an elderly heiress dies, she leaves everything to her assistant, Lucy. The heiress's nephew may have his own fortune, but he won't allow a con artist to dupe his family...even if he also wants her in his bed!

#2573 HIS TEMPTATION, HER SECRET
Whiskey Bay Brides • by Barbara Dunlop

When banker TJ learns he's donated bone marrow to his secret son, he proposes a marriage of convenience to handle the medical bills. But there's unfinished business between him and his new wife, the wallflower-turned-beauty he'd shared one passionate night with years ago...

#2574 BETWEEN MARRIAGE AND MERGER
The Locke Legacy • by Karen Booth

Billionaire businessman Noah Locke's fake engagement will solve his professional problems...and his fiancée in name only is the one woman he's wanted for years. But when the stakes rise, will their intense attraction end in disaster...or the truest merger of all?

Get 2 Free Books,
Plus 2 Free Gifts—
just for trying the Reader Service!

*Billionaire Broderick Steele was raised to hate his rival,
Glenna Mikkelson-Powers—even if she's the sexiest woman he's
ever known. Then, amid corporate mergers and scandal, they
find an abandoned baby who could be Broderick's...or Glenna's.
Playing house has never been so high stakes!*

*Read on for a sneak peek of
THE BABY CLAIM
by USA TODAY bestselling author Catherine Mann,
the first book in the ALASKAN OIL BARONS saga!*

Being so close to this man had never been a wise idea.

The sensual draw was too strong for any woman to resist for
long and stay sane. Broderick's long wool duster over his suit was
pure Hugo Boss. But the cowboy hat and leather boots had a hint of
wear that only increased his appeal. His dark hair, which attested to
his quarter-Inuit heritage, showed the first signs of premature gray.
His charisma and strength were as vast as the Alaskan tundra they
both called home.

In a state this large, there should have been enough space for
both of them. Theoretically, they should never have to cross paths.
But their feuding families' constant battle over dominance of the
oil industry kept Glenna Mikkelson-Powers and Broderick Steele
in each other's social circles.

Too often for her peace of mind.

Even so, he'd never shown up at her office before.

Light caught the mischief in his eyes, bringing out whiskey
tones in the dark depths. His full lips pulled upward in a haughty
smile.

"You're being highly unprofessional." She narrowed her own
eyes, angry at her reaction to him as she drank in his familiar
arrogance.

Their gazes held and the air crackled. She remembered the feeling all too well from their *Romeo and Juliet* fling in college.

Doomed from the start.

He was her rival. His mesmerizing eyes and broody disposition would not distract her.

She jabbed a manicured finger in his direction. "Your father is up to something."

She scooped up a brass paperweight in the shape of a bear that had belonged to her father. Shifting it from hand to hand was an oddly comforting ritual. Or perhaps not so odd. When she was a small girl, her father had told her the statue gave people power, attributing his success to the brass bear. After the last year of loss, Glenna needed every ounce of luck and power she could get.

"There's no need to threaten me with your version of brass knuckles." Humor left his face and his expression became all business. "But since you're as bemused by what's happening as I am, come with me to speak to your mother."

"Of course. Let's do that. We'll have this sorted out in no time." The sooner the better.

She wanted Broderick Steele out of her office and not a simple touch away.

Don't miss
THE BABY CLAIM
by USA TODAY *bestselling author Catherine Mann,*
the first book in the **ALASKAN OIL BARONS** *saga!*
Available February 2018
wherever Harlequin® Desire books and ebooks are sold.

And then follow the continuing story of two merging oil families competing to win in business...and in love—

THE DOUBLE DEAL
Available March 2018

THE LOVE CHILD
Available April 2018

THE TWIN BIRTHRIGHT
Available May 2018

www.Harlequin.com